THE PARADISE ROW GANG

THE PARADISE ROW GANG

Veronica Heley

Scripture Union
130 City Road, London EC1V 2NJ

By the same author
Swift Books
Genius at Work
Sky High

Leopard Books
Free-wheeling
Hawkeye of Paradise Row

Tiger Books
Good for Kate!

For 6–8s
Natasha's Badge
Natasha's Swing

First published 1989

ISBN 0 86201 570 7

Phototypeset by Input Typesetting Ltd, London
Printed and bound in Great Britain by Cox and Wyman Ltd, Reading

1

'No-one could say I scare easy . . .' said Fats.

'True,' said Toby, looking up at his big black friend with respect and admiration.

'. . . but do I see trouble? Or do I see trouble!'

Toby had sharp eyes which had earned him the nick-name of Hawkeye, but he didn't need sharp eyes to see they were being followed by a couple of baddies.

'Is discretion the better part of valour?' said Fats, hesitating at the corner of an alley. They were heavily into Shakespeare this term, and as their teacher had pointed out, Shakespeare covered most situations, including the appearance of baddies on the horizon.

'Are we mice or men?' said Toby. 'Let's run!' He led the way into the alley.

'Too late!' said Fats, as the third member of the gang cut off their line of retreat.

As luck would have it, the alley was deserted. The two boys were pushed against the wall, and Mike, who was the leader of the villains, trod on Toby's feet. Toby winced. Lewis, who was even bigger and blacker than Fats, did a dancing step around him, grinning fit to bust. The boys knew he liked hurting people.

'I owe you a lot more than that!' said Mike, 'Inter-fering in my business. I don't like little boys getting in my way. You hear me?'

Toby grimaced. He wasn't a big strong lad like Fats. Toby was fair-haired and slender. In fact, his mum said that on a clear day you could see right through him. That summer Mike and his gang had had a lot of fun, mugging and robbing more or less as they pleased. Toby and Fats and their friends had organised a trap and photographed the baddies in the act. Everyone had been really pleased to see Mike and his friends arrested. Even Skinny, Mike's younger brother, had been pleased. But something had gone wrong when the baddies appeared in court, and now they were out on bail and twice as dangerous.

Mike said, 'Afraid of me, are you? Good! Now I don't bear you no grudge for what's past. They couldn't make it stick when we come up in court, and they won't in future, neither. But what I want to make clear is, you keep out of my territory in future, or else!'

Toby was glad Mike didn't want to tear him apart, but didn't understand the reference to his 'territory'.

'The Wasteland, Dumbo,' said Mike. 'Where you had your adventure playground. Where the church used to be. You and your lot had your fun there this summer. Now I'm taking over. Understand?'

Toby wanted to say it wasn't theirs to take over. He wanted to defy Mike. But somehow the words wouldn't come. He nodded. He didn't mean to. His head just did it, all by itself. Fats nodded, too.

Mike and his friends went off, laughing. Toby rubbed his feet, and tried to act like they didn't hurt. He thought they'd been outgunned. It was no shame to give in when you were outgunned.

After a while the two boys turned back into the street and went on down the road towards the block of flats which dominated Paradise Row. Fats lived in the flats, and so did Mike and Lewis. So did a lot of other people. Not many of them liked the flats, especially with Mike and Lewis around.

They crossed the road into the shadow of the church tower. The body of the church had disappeared in the bombing of 1944 and only the crypt and tower remained. The site had been a derelict Wasteland till that summer, when Toby's mother had teamed up with the local doctor to persuade the church people and the borough council to allow an adventure playground there. Now the children were back at school, and the Council men were removing their equipment.

Fats and Toby came to the gap in the boarding round the Wasteland and looked inside. The Wasteland had been their own special place; that, and the Lookout room up in the tower.

Now the ground lay beaten hard where the swings and ropes had been. On the site of the wooden hut used by the playleader, a small bonfire was burning rubbish. There wasn't anything much left to remind them what a splendid place it had been that summer.

The Wasteland was empty. Waiting.

'What would Mike want it for?' said Fats.

'We've got to stop him,' said Toby.

'How?' said Fats.

'Tell the doc. He'll know what to do.'

Toby and Fats admired their local doctor more than anyone in the world. He always had time for them, even though he was permanently overworked. He'd even taken time out to tell them stories about Jesus on Sundays in the summer. He was working to get the church reopened, but it was hard going.

'Is he still friends with your mum?' asked Fats, grinning.

'On and off,' said Toby, also grinning. His dad had been killed in an accident when he and his sister were small, and his mum had had a tough time working and raising two kids at the same time. She had a short fuse and wasn't the easiest person to be friends with. Luckily the doc seemed to like her, whatever she said or did.

It began to sleet, and they scooted for home. The first building they came to was the doc's surgery, and next came the door to the flat above, where Toby lived. Fats shouted that he'd be in touch, and dived down the next alley on his way to the flats, while Toby got out his front door key.

The doc drove up in a flurry of spray and squealing brakes. Toby waved like mad, but the doc was in a hurry, and rushed into the surgery without seeing him.

Toby went up the stairs, and paused to listen, and have a good sniff. He couldn't smell cooking, and he couldn't hear the telly, or his mum on the phone. That meant the flat was empty. If his twin sister Nikki had been around, the telly would have been on. If his mum had been around, there'd be something cooking, or she'd be on the phone.

There was a note from his mum in the kitchen.

'Gone shopping with Nikki. Important: THE WASTELAND IS OUT OF BOUNDS! Luv, Mum.'

Toby threw his school bag at the kitchen wall.

It really was the pits! First Mike and his gang, and now his mum. Why was it they always had to stop people enjoying themselves?

He sat down and thought about it. He couldn't go against his mum. It wasn't worth it. He could get the doc to keep Mike and his gang out of the Wasteland, but that might take time.

Meanwhile, he had to rescue his most precious possessions, which he'd left in the tower. During the war, the doc's grandfather had been an Air Raid Warden who had used the tower to watch out for bombs and fires. The Warden had left his binoculars and diary in the tower. Toby had found them, and used them to help trap Mike. It was unthinkable that these things should fall into Mike's hands now.

Toby went up the stairs to the top floor, where he had his bedroom. The first floor rooms looked onto the street at the front and onto a small paved yard at the back. Toby had one window which overlooked the yard, but he had another, bigger one at the side of the building. This second window overlooked the Wasteland and the church tower.

He looked out. The rain seemed to have set in for the evening. Soon it would be dark when they came home from school. The Wasteland looked drab and even menacing in the dusk. He repressed a shiver, telling himself that conditions were perfect.

Mike wasn't there. No-one was there.

No-one would see him if he slipped across now, before his mum and Nikki got back. Just to rescue his belongings. Besides, she hadn't actually said the tower was out of bounds. Only the Wasteland.

Toby knew that was fudged thinking, but he went, anyway. No one saw him scamper across the Wasteland. He went straight to the side door of the tower. It was locked, and someone had hammered a strong-looking hasp into the doorframe, and put a chain and padlock through it and the door handle. That was new, and pretty unfriendly, he thought.

Toby knew another way in, though. A secret way. Just above ground level in an inconspicuous corner nearby, there was a small window. Once it had had bars across but now it was secured against the weather only by a warped piece of plywood. Toby tugged it out, and slipped through into the darkness of the stairwell. He hadn't needed to get into the church this way for yonks, and it was a tight squeeze.

Standing up, he spotted something that shouldn't be there. He wasn't called Hawkeye for nothing. What he saw was an empty Coke tin. And a couple of cigarette butts. Someone had been in since the place had been cleaned up at the end of the summer holidays. Then he heard a tinny, scrabbling sound.

His chest went tight on him. He suffered from asthma, and although he hadn't been much troubled by it this summer, he could feel it hovering now.

He kept still, listening. Had a tramp got into the church? He looked up, to where the stairs went through a door into the tower. The sound hadn't come from above. It had come from the darkness below, from the crypt.

The crypt was a maze of gloomy caverns, interrupted at frequent intervals by large stone pillars. The adventure playground people had only used one central area on wet days, and warned the children not to go poking into odd corners. Funnily enough, no-one had particularly felt inclined to do so. It wasn't that sort of place.

Toby had seen a sketch plan of the crypt in the diary, and had thought about exploring one day. But he'd always put it off. He decided this was not the moment to start, either.

His straining ears caught another sound. Music. Rock music. And then the sound of a radio commercial blaring out.

Toby blinked. He'd been thinking about things even worse than stray tramps; about ghosts and things that go bump in the night. But neither tramps nor ghosts usually operated radios.

Could it be Mike down there? If so, someone ought to be told about it.

Toby thought that if he crept down, quietly, a step at a time, he could peep round the corner and see who it was. If it was Mike, then Toby would have a head start on getting away. Mike was big and heavy. Mike wasn't expecting to be spied on.

Down and down Toby went, taking care not to make even the slightest of scuffling sounds. There was a grille across the entrance to the crypt but it was ajar. Toby edged through and came to a bend in the passage which led into the big central room. He got an eye to the corner and nearly collapsed, he was so relieved at what he saw.

One of his own special friends was there, sitting on an improvised bed, tipping back a can of Coke, and listening to the radio.

'Hi, Skinny!' said Toby. 'What are you doing here?'

2

Skinny dropped his can of Coke with a crash. He ducked into the nearest dark corner, hunching himself over as if expecting to be kicked.

Toby said, 'Hey! Skinny! It's me. Toby. What's the matter?'

Skinny peered out, still crouching. His face gleamed bone white with fear.

'I thought it was . . .'

'Mike?' said Toby. He knew Skinny was scared of Mike. Everyone was scared of Mike. Mike had given his old mum a couple of knocks that summer, and Skinny had been living in fear all this time, wondering when Mike would find out that his young brother had helped Toby stop the muggings.

'Mike's found out?' said Toby, looking over his shoulder. There was nothing but blackness behind him, and nothing but blackness beyond the light of the bicycle lamp Skinny had set up on a chair nearby. The chair was a rickety one, a throw-out. There was a pile of cardboard cartons on the stone floor nearby, and a sleeping bag on top of that. Plus the radio. And that was all.

Toby said, 'You've run away? Well, I don't blame you, but you can't stay here. Couldn't you go to the police?'

Skinny cowered even lower, and Toby put a hand on his friend's shoulder. 'All right. I know Mike would take it out on you and your mum if you went to the police. But you can't stay here for long. I mean, it's so . . .'

Skinny cleared his throat. 'It's a bit scary, but better than . . . you don't know what he's like.'

'But what about food, and school and clothes and

things? I'd take you home with me, only mum would make you go to the police, so that won't do.'

'Just for a few days,' said Skinny. 'He's going away, then, and everything'll be all right. You won't give me away, will you?'

'No fear! But won't he guess? He's just warned me and Fats off the Wasteland. I only came in to get my binoculars and the diary. Mum's forbidden me to come here, too. There's no-one going to be around in the day-time, because we're all back at school.'

Toby could feel Skinny shivering beside him. Skinny was bigger than Toby, but someone had been hitting him pretty hard. He'd got a black eye, and a nasty graze on his chin.

Toby said, 'Well, I suppose, come to think of it, that you're safer here than most places. No-one would think of looking for you here, especially Mike. I mean, he might want to make himself a den or something in the Wasteland, but he's not likely to come in here. He's not exactly a church-goer, is he?'

Skinny didn't even smile.

Toby scanned the darkly shadowed spaces around them.

'It is a spooky place, I suppose. But look at it this way, if there is a spook here, it'll only be the Warden, and he looks just like the doc, and no-one could be afraid of him. I saw him in a dream, once. He loved this place. I used to think he haunted it, but that's all nonsense, of course. But if he did, then he'd be good to have on your side, wouldn't he?'

Skinny didn't seem much comforted.

Toby sighed. 'What about food? Shall I bring you something tonight? It's raining, but I suppose I could make some excuse, bring you something from the chippie.'

Skinny said, 'Here, I've got some money. Chips, and some more Coke to drink, if you can manage it.'

'Can do. Something to read?'

Skinny said he had some magazines, and didn't fancy school work. 'But will you swear not to tell? Not even Fats!'

'I won't swear,' said Toby. 'And I'll have to tell Fats. He won't grass on you, you know he won't. Between us, we can get you food and that. OK?'

'It's only for a few days,' said Skinny, gulping, and looking over Toby's shoulder. 'Tell you what; I'll get your binoculars down from the tower when it's light. You can't go up there now, in the dark. I'll have them ready for you when you bring me something after school tomorrow.'

'Right,' said Toby. 'Thanks.' Only after he'd left the church, carefully pushing the board back into place over the broken window, did he remember that he'd need the diary as well. He'd tell Skinny about that, later. Meanwhile, he'd got to find an excuse to go out again that evening. It might take some doing, the weather having turned nasty.

As he climbed the stairs to the flat, he smelled curry. That was good. He could also smell a cigar. His mum smoked, on and off. When she was worried or het up about something she smoked quite a lot, but only cigarettes. The doc didn't smoke at all.

Toby knew only one person who smoked cigars, and that was the Awful Jeff, his mum's friend from the council. Toby didn't reckon much to the bearded Jeff person. Neither did Nikki. But their mum seemed to find him amusing from time to time.

Yes, there he was, large as life if not larger, definitely growing a paunch, and looking as if he'd been sitting in the chair at the top of the kitchen table for yonks.

Toby's twin sister Nikki, who was as dark and sturdy as he was fair and slim, was trying to make herself inconspicuous in a corner. That was a laugh. Nikki stood out in a crowd, like their mum. Toby could see that Nikki was upset about something, even from where he stood in the doorway.

Kate Webb ran her hands up through her short dark hair and said to Toby. 'You're late. Where have you been?'

'Yes, how come you're so late?' said the Beard, following Kate's lead.

'Great news, Toby!' said his mum, with a flirty look at the Awful Jeff. 'There's going to be a vacancy on the council, and Jeff thinks I ought to stand.'

Toby looked at Nikki, who responded with a grimace. Nikki might look like her mum, but she didn't go for her mum's taste in men. Both Nikki and Toby preferred the doc, and Kate had seemed to prefer him of late, too.

'Oh,' said Toby, ignoring the whole question of his lateness, 'Won't standing for the Council mean a lot of extra word, unpaid?' Kate worked for the council as a Youth and Community Worker, and she worked hard, but the pay was not marvellous.

'It's a great honour,' said Kate, sharply stirring the curry, 'and a chance to change the system. I'm not afraid of hard work.'

'Unlike some people,' said Jeff, with meaning.

'*I* don't think the doc's let us down,' said Nikki, carrying on a conversation interrupted by Toby's entrance.

'What do you know about it?' said their mum, clashing plates onto the table. 'Toby, wash your hands, they're filthy. Jeff, you'll join us for supper, won't you? The doc sometimes joins us on a Tuesday evening, but after what's happened, I told him not to bother.'

'What has happened, then?' said Toby.

'The crypt,' said Kate to Toby. 'The church people have turned down my scheme for a community centre in the crypt.'

Nikki intervened. 'They haven't turned it down. The doc said they liked the idea, but there's lots of things wrong that would have to be put right and it would cost a lot of money. Things like,' she read from a note which had been left open on the table, ' "rewiring, new heating, fire doors, and toilets and ramps for disabled people." The doc said he was going to get the quotes, to see how much it would cost. . .'

'I know when I'm being given the run-around,' said Kate. 'The doc's just making noises. He isn't really going to do anything. Jeff says there's a developer just itching to get his hands on the site. The church people'll make a mint, and build lots of town houses for yuppies. What do they care about the people who live here!'

'Hear, hear!' said Jeff. 'You've got to force them to recognise the rights of the people, you've got to bring them to their knees, and only then will you get them to do something . . .'

'Come the revolution, they'll all be hanging from the lamp-posts,' said Toby, more or less under his breath.

'What was that?' said Kate, going pink. 'You know nothing about it. Now eat your supper and no more nonsense. The Wasteland's out of bounds in future, and so is the tower. You hear me?'

'I left my binoculars there,' said Toby, 'and the diary. I'll have to fetch them.'

'Then you'll have to ask the churchwarden to get them for you. I won't have you going there again. Understand?'

Toby kept his eyes down on his plate. Helping Skinny was going to be even more difficult than he'd thought.

Luckily, after supper Jeff took Kate off to a meeting and Nikki started on her homework in front of the TV, dividing her attention between 'EastEnders' and geography. She could do that. Toby couldn't, and always did his homework up at the top of the house in his own room. So it wasn't difficult for him to time his exit from the flat when Nikki wouldn't notice.

He borrowed her pocket torch and slipped out, only to run straight into the doc who was coming out of his surgery. The doc worked all hours, and it wasn't unusual to see him there at that time, but Toby went beetroot.

He really liked the doc, and he hated to think there'd been a row between the doc and his mum. He didn't know what to do about it.

The doc knew. 'Ah, Toby; just the person I need. You know Mr Gaunt, the churchwarden? Lives at number 42. Fell down the stairs at the church today. Nothing broken, but badly shaken up. He's home now but his wife tells me he's fretting about the church. He asked for you. Could you make time to pop in and see him?'

'Asked for me?' Toby blinked. He knew Mr Gaunt, of course. They'd always called him the Cheshire Cat, because he had a great big grin when he was pleased, and his mouth turned right down when he wasn't. The effect was a bit off-putting till you got to know him.

The doc looked at his watch, unlocked his car, and threw his bag in. 'Asked for you, that's right. Something about your binoculars. Had you left them there? Wants to see you. Can do?'

'Can do,' said Toby, glad to find that whatever his mum had been up to, the doc wasn't going to give him the old heave ho.

'This evening, if you can. Then he might sleep . . .' said the doc, starting up the car, and slamming the door. He looked over his shoulder and drove off into a narrow gap in the traffic.

Toby tried not to worry about his homework as he fetched the chips and Coke and wriggled his way into the tower. This time he couldn't see any light, or hear any music. He went down cautiously, to find Skinny sitting with his finger on the volume control of the radio, and the lamp half hidden under a blanket.

'Here,' said Toby. 'Got to run. Anything else you want? I think Mr Gaunt's got my binoculars. See you tomorrow after school with some more food. OK?'

Skinny nodded, and started on the chips while Toby rushed back up the stairs. It was really dark on the stairs. He'd have been lost without the torch.

The streets were shiny and black in the rain, but the wind had dropped. Toby found No. 42 Paradise Row, which was in one of the terraces of older houses still standing. Mrs Gaunt opened the door and ushered him upstairs, saying perhaps her old man would get some peace now Toby had come.

The bedroom was papered with heavy-headed roses, and crowded with old-fashioned, dark furniture. The bed was high off the floor and the Gaunts weren't into modern duvets. A counterpane was on top of an eider-down on top of blankets over the frail body of Mr Gaunt. His shoulders were all strapped up and his face was bruised. He was uneasily asleep when Toby entered, but woke with a start and looked as if he didn't know where he was.

Toby wasn't sure what to say or do. He said, 'Hello, Mr Gaunt. You wanted me for something?'

'What?' said the old man, irritably. 'I didn't ask for you. Who says I did, eh?'

Mrs Gaunt said, soothingly, 'You told the doctor you wanted to see young Toby. Don't you remember? Something about the tower. . .'

'I don't remember that,' declared Mr Gaunt. 'What I want to know is . . . Who pushed me down the stairs, eh?'

'Now, now,' said Mrs Gaunt. 'There's no need to talk like that. No-one pushed you. You slipped and fell. Nothing's broken, and you'll soon be up and about again . . .'

'I know what I'm saying!' said Mr Gaunt, irritably. 'I went up to check that the roof wasn't leaking . . . after the bomb, you know . . . they patched it up, but . . .'

Mrs Gaunt sighed and gave Toby a warning shake of her head. Her husband was clearly wandering in his mind, and no wonder, after such a shake-up.

'. . . then I heard someone behind me, and the next thing I knew I was being pushed down the stairs. It's a miracle I wasn't killed . . . then I don't remember . . .

how did I get to hospital . . . the keys!'

He sat upright, and tried to get out of bed, but failed.

'The keys are perfectly all right,' said Mrs Gaunt, pushing him back under the covers. 'Lie back and close your eyes. I'll find your keys for you. And perhaps Toby can drop in again tomorrow, to see how you are.'

'The keys . . .' muttered Mr Gaunt, but obediently closed his eyes and dozed off.

Mrs Gaunt put her finger to her lips, and led Toby downstairs. 'I'm afraid you've had a wasted journey.'

'I thought maybe he'd got my binoculars, which I left in the tower.'

'He hadn't got any binoculars on him when they brought him home, that I can tell you. Nor his keys. Him and that church. It'll be the death of him, I've often said so. Going out in all weathers, and all hours of the day and night. And what for, I say. It isn't as if he gets paid for it.'

'You don't really think he could have been pushed, do you?'

'Heavens, no.'

'But the keys are missing?'

'I expect whoever picked him up has the keys. I expect it was the doc.'

'Thanks,' said Toby. 'I'll check and drop by tomorrow, put his mind at rest. Is there anything else I can do?'

Mrs Gaunt said, 'I'll let you know,' and showed him out into the street, slamming the door behind her. She was a grim-looking woman with a nutcracker jaw, probably due to badly fitting false teeth. It was said it took an earthquake to make her smile.

Toby hunched his shoulders against the rain and set off back home. At this rate he'd be enrolling full time as a social worker, without pay – like Mr Gaunt.

3

On his way to school next day, Toby dropped into the surgery. The receptionist took a message from Toby about the keys. She was new to the job, and looked flustered. Toby wondered if she'd remember to tell the doc. It was important.

Detouring round the block, Toby tried the official front door of the church under the tower. It was very firmly locked. Mr Gaunt must have locked it behind him when he went into the tower, and then fallen and . . . But who had helped him up and called the doc to his rescue? It might be worth enquiring. Keys shouldn't be allowed to fall into the wrong hands.

At lunch Toby took Fats into a quiet corner behind the science labs, and told him about Skinny, and about the quarrel between the doc and his mum, and about Mr Gaunt's fall. Fats nodded, and said it took some thinking about.

So they sat there and thought. It was a bit draughty at the back of the science labs, but it wasn't drizzling much, and it was quiet.

'Tell you what,' said Toby, 'I'm really sorry for Skinny. And helping him will be getting back at Mike.'

'Sure,' said Fats, 'but shouldn't we tell someone? The doc, perhaps?'

'Not if it's only for a few days. Think of a life without Mike. Pure bliss.'

'There's a rumour in the flats that he's up to something. Something with loadsa money in it. Secret. Not mugging, like usual. Something big. Lewis and the other one, Ricky, they're in it, too. Ricky's been boasting. Going on his holidays, he says, somewhere warm.'

'Good riddance. I don't like to think of them taking over the Wasteland, even though we can't use it at the moment. Somehow it's all wrong.'

'Invasion of the Daleks?'

'Yeah, that's exactly what it feels like.'

There was silence for a while. Then Toby said, 'What I really don't like, is what Jeff says about the church and the Wasteland maybe going to a developer.'

'Yeah. I can see they'd make a mint . . .'

'But what about us? There isn't another church for miles . . .'

'I don't feel I'm strong enough, or good enough to keep going without a church, without someone to show me the way.'

'We need petrol . . .'

'. . . topping up . . .'

'We need the doc to tell us what to do.'

'So let's ask him, shall we?'

Going home, they paused at the entrance to the Wasteland, to stare at something new. Where there'd only been a flat space yesterday, was a shack built of this and that, of corrugated iron, of pieces of packing and planks of rotting wood taken from skips.

Fats chanted, 'By the pricking of my thumbs,
Something wicked this way scrams . . .'

'It's like magic,' said Toby. 'It wasn't here yesterday, and now it is. No prizes for guessing who put it up.'

Lewis, the big black bloke, came out of the shack and leaned against it, lighting up a fag. He looked at the two boys and they politely faded into the distance.

'Possession is nine tenths of the law,' said Fats. 'It's going to take an army to get rid of them.'

'It's only for a few days,' said Toby, trying hard to believe it. 'But how are we going to get food to Skinny, with them sitting in the Wasteland?'

'A horse, a horse! My kingdom for a horse!' said Fats.

Toby walloped Fats with his school bag, and they both laughed so much they didn't notice the doc open his car door and step out in front of them.

'Watch it!' said the doc, grinning. 'Or I'll have the pair of you up for grievous bodily harm.'

'Hi!' said Toby, 'We were coming to see you . . .'

'Can't stop!' said the doc, looking at his watch. 'But ditto, lads. We must talk, have another session at the church, Sunday, same time. Bring your friends. Did you see Mr Gaunt? Is he all right? I haven't had time to pop in today, but . . . Must dash! Spread the word, won't you?'

He vanished into the surgery with a swish and a bang of the door, leaving the two boys to gape after him.

'Well, we couldn't stop him now, not with a surgery full of people waiting for him,' said Fats.

'No, but . . .'

'Mm. But. What do we do now?'

'Get some food for Skinny. I've got an idea how to get it to him. Mike's shack is right where he can see anyone enter the Wasteland from the street, but the side door and the secret window are round the corner. If you give me a leg up, I can get over the broken bit of hoarding where that lorry ran into it, and I don't think they'd see me.'

'I don't think I could get through that little window,' said Fats, surveying himself. 'But I can chuck you over all right, and stand guard till you get back . . . and if they spot you I'll run and get help. Right?'

Toby gulped. 'Right,' he said, and tried a whistle on for size. He'd heard whistling helped, when you were scared.

'You're doing what?' said Kate, arms akimbo and hair standing on end.

'The doc said he'd have a meeting at the church on Sunday, and I'm going to it with Fats.'

'You'll do nothing of the kind. I want you to help me, Sunday. I've got a mountain of leaflets to deliver . . .'

'I'll help you,' said Nikki, in her silkiest voice. She

smiled up at Jeff. 'At least, I would if only my shoes didn't leak. You see, I've only got this one pair of trainers and . . .'

Toby went beetroot red. Nikki had several pairs of trainers, all in good nick. Nikki liked shoes. He sometimes thought it was the only feminine thing about her. She liked to wear jeans and sweaters, or boiler suits all the time . . . finished off with a pair of really good boots. Nikki's idea of luxury would be a wardrobe full of really good shoes and boots.

Kate ground her teeth, but Jeff was stupid enough to fall for it. 'I'll help you buy some more shoes,' he said. 'If you help your mum deliver leaflets, of course you should get paid for it.'

Kate looked as if she didn't know whether to smile or scream, so lit up a ciggie instead. Nikki looked pleased. Toby scowled, thinking that the doc wouldn't have been taken in so easily. The doc liked Nikki, but he didn't let her walk all over him. It was another count against the Beard.

'That's settled, then,' said Kate. 'Sunday morning we deliver leaflets, and have a committee meeting after. I'll want you kids to hand round tea and biscuits.'

'Sorry,' said Toby. 'I'll deliver leaflets any other time, but not Sunday morning.'

Jeff said, all roguish humour, 'You mean it actually wants to go to church?'

'Yes,' said Toby. 'I do.'

'How about that!' said the Beard, looking down on Toby as if examining a specimen at the zoo. 'I didn't think his sort still existed.'

'We may be rare,' said Toby, 'but we're not extinct.'

'Har har,' said the Beard. 'It bites, does it?'

This was a shade too much for Kate. 'Oh that's enough, Jeff. He takes after his father. If Toby wants to go to church, then let him. It can't do any harm, after all.'

Nikki looked as if she were coming to the boil. She

might disagree with almost everything Toby did, but she hated to have him attacked by outsiders.

Toby said quickly, before Nikki could lose her temper, or his mum change her mind, 'Well, that's all right, then. I'll start delivering tonight.'

'What about your own shoes?' said Kate, stubbing out one cigarctte and lighting another.

Toby felt himself swell with love for her. His mum knew his shoes were getting to the point of no return. They both knew there wasn't enough money in the kitty that month to buy him new ones. She knew it wasn't fair that Nikki should grab everything, and she was trying to make it up to him, to give him the opportunity to get the money from Jeff.

'Sure,' said Jeff, though he didn't say it with any great enthusiasm. 'Only fair.'

Suddenly Toby realised he couldn't possibly let Jeff buy him anything.

'No!' said Toby. 'I don't need any shoes!' He rushed out of the room and up the stairs to his room. His chest was tight and painful. He could hear himself wheezing like an old man. He hadn't had an asthma attack in ages, but this had all the signs of being a beaut.

He found his inhaler, and got down to it. His mum came up and stood in the doorway, watching him, fiddling with her ciggie. He tried to pretend she wasn't there. He wasn't up to arguing with her about the shoes. He knew he'd been rude to Jeff. He couldn't help it. He just didn't like the Beard.

If it had been the doc who'd offered to help buy some shoes, well, that would have been different, somehow.

Toby felt bruised inside. He wished his mum would go away. He felt he might say something stupid and rude to her, too, if he wasn't very careful.

She said, 'I'll tell Jeff you're not well, and won't be doing any delivering of leaflets tonight.'

'I said I'd do it,' said Toby, between his teeth. 'And I will!'

His mum opened her mouth to say something, probably about Jeff being a really nice chap when you got to know him. Toby turned his back on her, and after a moment she went away.

He looked out of the window. Grey, grey, grey. Grey smoke drifted up past his window from the shack down below in the Wasteland.

Occupied Territory.

Danger.

Keep Out.

All the world was grey. Jeff had brought the greyness even inside the flat where usually it was pretty good. Toby could feel it was grey inside himself, too.

He wished he were dead. Even the doc was no help, now.

4

Fats said, 'Do you like it?'

Toby knew he oughtn't to, but he grinned. Fats was a wizard with the spray can, and this was one of his best efforts. The letters were huge and the message could be read even from the flats.

THE FUTURE
HERE – SUNDAY – 10.30
DON'T MISS IT!

He'd sprayed the words over a cigarette advert on the hoarding round the Wasteland. Fats wasn't into smoking.

'It's pretty neat, if I say so myself,' said Fats. 'I told Red and the other members of the gang to come. And to tell their parents.'

They heard a shout, and Nikki ran up with her best friend, Jan. 'Why didn't you wait for me?'

'Thought you were going swimming,' said Toby, carefully not reminding her what she usually said about church being boring.

Nikki said, 'You should have seen Jeff's face, when I thanked him for the boots and then said I'd give them their first airing at church and deliver leaflets this afternoon!'

She gave Toby a wicked grin, and ran on ahead to disappear through the open main door of the church. Toby and Fats hung back, watching to see who else was likely to come. Some of their friends did, and some of their friends' parents. Not Skinny, of course. Their friend Red came and his dad, known as Mr Red because he had red hair, too. There were old men and women, breathing heavily as they hauled themselves up the steps and into the church. Younger women with children. People they knew, and people they didn't.

'The power of the media!' said Fats. 'You simply gotta advertise, these days.'

'We'll miss Mr Gaunt. I popped in to see him. He's still in bed. Doesn't know what day of the week it is, half the time.'

They turned into the church and made their way to chairs at the back. Mrs Gaunt was there, wearing what looked like a blue hedgehog on her head, and brandishing the church keys with an air of importance.

The doc wasn't there, yet, but everyone was behaving as if this was a proper church, sitting up straight, and muttering to one another rather than chatting.

Mrs Fats was sitting in the front row in her Sunday best, with all five of Fats' brothers beside her, in descending order of height.

Fats said, 'I told her I was definitely coming here, and she said she'd bring all of us, provided we all went with her to the other church this evening. Two services in a day, groan, groan!'

'I'm late, I'm late, for a very important date!' hissed Fats, as the doc dashed in, looking even more harassed than usual.

'What?' said Toby.

'The White Rabbit. Alice in Wonderland. I'm late, I'm late . . .'

'Off with his head!' responded Toby, remembering the Red Queen's favourite instruction.

Mrs Fats turned round and gave them a look. They straightened out their faces and sat upright. Everyone looked attentively at the doc, who looked shattered.

The doc had his bag with him. When had he not got his bag with him? He scrabbled around in it, and when he couldn't find what he was looking for, he stopped and stared down at his hands.

Toby thought, Why, he's praying for help . . . Toby had a moment of confusion when he wondered what they were all doing there, and then he began to pray, too. Everyone stopped shifting around, and a lovely, prayerful silence filled the maimed church.

The doc lifted his head after a while, and said, 'I'd madc some notes. I thought this was going to be an ordinary sort of meeting, just to tell you what's been happening, and what's been planned. But I've mislaid my notes, and perhaps that's as well. We can't have a meeting in a church and leave God out of it, can we? So let us, each one of us, ask God to help us. In silence . . .'

The wonderful, prayerful silence went on. Toby, shooting glances out of the corners of his eyes, saw that everyone was wearing the same kind of intent expression.

'And now,' said the doc. 'How about a good rousing chorus or hymn? I know we've got no organ or piano but I think we could make some sort of joyful noise, couldn't we? How about "One more step along the world I go . . ." Because that's what it's all about, isn't it? Taking one step at a time.'

Mrs Fats hummed out a great bell of a note, and everyone started off, pretty raggedly at first, and not always knowing the words though it was something the children had learned at school, but all joining in the chorus when they got to it. What's more, they all stood up to sing, and some of them even clapped to it . . . and not only Mrs Fats was clapping by the end.

Then everyone sat down and looked at the doc.

He'd forgotten his nerves by this time. He said, 'Well, I daresay you've heard that things have been moving, lately. If the church authorities ever did have any idea that this church was dead and could be neatly tidied away . . . well, they've stopped thinking that way now. The problem is, it would cost an enormous amount to rebuild the church as it was, and there aren't enough churchgoers around here to justify doing that.

'The next idea was to pull it down – what's left of it

– and build an old people's home, or sheltered accommodation, perhaps with a small chapel in it. A lot of people like that idea.

'Then Mrs Webb, whom I'm sure you all know, our Youth and Community Worker, wants us to pull this building down and build a community centre, and there's no doubt we could do with one . . .'

Toby nudged Fats and gestured with his head. A small pallid face was peering round the door that led to the stairs and the crypt. Skinny. Poor Skinny. Toby sent Skinny a smile, but didn't get one back.

'. . . and the last alternative – the one I like best – is that we keep the crypt for use as a community centre during the week, and use the tower as a church on Sundays. I'd like to turn the Wasteland into a community garden, with proper seats and maybe a small area for children's playing equipment. That would be the cheapest solution, but it would still cost a lot of money because the place has to be rewired, and replumbed and decorated, and fire doors put in, and all the safety regulations met. I'm getting quotes for all this, and soon maybe we'll know how much . . .'

Skinny's face slowly lowered itself and then became stationary. He was sitting down, where he could hear, but couldn't be seen except by Fats and Toby on the opposite side.

'Are there any questions?' said the doc, and of course there were, all boringly preoccupied with money and committee work. Toby could see that the grown-ups were going to spend hours arguing about the situation. He began to shift, and so did Fats, and the others. The doc held up his hand, and smiled at them.

'I've just been reminded that this isn't the time or place to talk about money. I'll set up a meeting at the surgery one evening, and we'll go into ways and means, but for now, there's a story I'd like to tell you.

'Once there was a rabbit, living in a comfortable hole and doing no particular harm to anyone. Every day he would go out for a walk and pass the time of day with his friends. But one day when he got back to his hole, he found someone else had moved in. A loud and fierce voice came from the hole, saying that he, the intruder, killed and ate a hundred rabbits before breakfast.

'The rabbit was frightened, and went to fetch his friend the dog to help him. The intruder told the dog that he killed and ate a hundred dogs every day before breakfast, and the dog was frightened away, too. The rabbit fetched increasingly large and ferocious animals to deal with the intruder, but all were frightened away.

'At his wits' end, the rabbit told his story to a frog, who said he knew how to deal with the intruder. The frog hopped to the hole, and the intruder, in his great, fierce voice, started to say that he killed and ate a hundred frogs for break. . . And at that point the frog shot out his tongue, flicked the intruder from the roof, and ate it.

'You see,' said the doc, 'the intruder was only a fly, but it was a fly who could magnify and project his voice.' He looked around at them, smiling. 'Would anyone like to give the fly a name?'

Toby thought, The doc knows all about Mike, and how we've been warned off the Wasteland.

'Yes,' said Toby, 'The fly's name is Fear.'

'And who was the frog?'

'Jesus?' said Red, rather doubtfully. It did seem a bit much to call Jesus a frog.

'Nearly,' said the doc, laughing. 'How about "Trust in Jesus"? If we trust in him, and are doing his will, then what's the point of being afraid? Fears magnify until they seem unconquerable. But they aren't. And if we go about our lives doing what we know is right, and remembering to ask Jesus for his help, then even if we do come across things which frighten us, somehow when it comes to the crunch, the thing we've been so afraid of turns out to be not nearly as dreadful as we'd thought . . . or it even disappears altogether. Are you with me?'

'Yes!' said Toby and Fats, and a lot of the others nodded their heads. They all looked smiley and serene.

Then an awful thing happened.

The outer door of the church opened with a bang and Kate Webb stalked into the church.

She said, 'If you're having a meeting about the future of this place, I do think I ought to have been invited.'

'Take a seat,' said the doc, still smiling. 'We have been talking about the future of the church, but nothing's settled yet and I'll be setting up a proper meeting soon to . . .'

'Did you tell them about the developer?' said Kate, not accepting the invitation to take a seat. Toby shifted uneasily. He could see she was furious about something.

The doc stopped smiling. 'I did hear a rumour that a developer was interested, but I'm sure the church authorities wouldn't . . .'

'Of course they would! They'd clear a million, selling out to the yuppies, and we could cry for our community centre till . . .'

'Look,' said the doc, being patient, but showing signs of anger, 'I believe you are wrong, but in any case, this is neither the time nor the place to . . .'

'Where better? And why not now? I want to make it quite clear that . . .'

'Missus,' said Mrs Fats, with the commanding air of a queen, 'you're out of order. This is a church meeting, to talk to God, and hear the Good News. You want to talk politics, you go somewheres else.'

'That's right!' said some. And, 'Very true . . .' But others shifted in their seats, and looked more at Kate than at the doc.

'I think,' said the doc, 'we'd better close with a prayer . . .'

'I think,' interrupted Kate, 'that we'd better *start* with a plan of action. If we don't all get together and do something, then we're going to lose our community centre. How dare they plot to deprive us of . . .'

Mrs Fats rose to her feet, all fifteen stone of her, and faced Kate. 'Missus,' said Mrs Fats, 'How you gonna lose something you never had? You got no rights to tell the church people anything. You think they're stupid, or something?'

'Let her speak . . .'

'But she's got no right to . . .'

'Silence!' said the doc, in a voice which produced a brittle moment of quiet. There was colour in the doc's cheeks, and he looked taller than usual. He said, 'I know that Mrs Webb cares deeply for the well-being of our people. Perhaps she has expressed herself too strongly . . .'

'I meant every word that I . . .'

'. . . and I will call another meeting at the surgery, where we can discuss the whole matter. But for now, let us thank God for being with us, and ask him to bless us in the coming days . . . to guide our steps . . . in the name of Jesus. Amen.'

Mrs Fats barely waited for the 'amen' before she swept out of church with her family. The others all piled out, too, talking, arguing, taking sides. Kate looked right through the doc and stormed out, taking Nikki with her. The doc was buttonholed by Mrs Gaunt and some of the older, more thoughtful members of the congregation, but Toby slipped to the door leading to the crypt where Skinny was beckoning to him from behind a pillar.

'I gotta talk to you!' hissed Skinny, shrinking back into the shadows. 'I don't want you coming round any more! It's not safe! Tell Fats! I got enough food. Me mum brought me some. Just . . . keep away. Right?'

'But Skinny, why? What's happened? You're shivering. Are you ill? Let me tell the doc, and . . .'

'No, don't! I'm all right, I tell you. And it'll only be for a couple days. It's just that . . . I seen him, the ghost you told me about! The old man, the Warden. He don't like being disturbed, people coming into his church. He said, "Tell everyone to keep away, or else!" I tell you, he's horrible! He's the worst thing I ever saw in my whole life!'

5

Toby got together with Fats that evening, on pretext of sharing a book for homework.

'. . . and Skinny really was frightened, Fats. He was shaking all over. He skittered off down the stairs before I could get anything else out of him. Then the doc shouted that they wanted to lock up, and I had to go.'

They looked out of Toby's window, over the Wasteland. Smoke rose hazily from the shack where Mike and his gang were hanging out, and because there was no wind, the smoke hung around and spread out, creating a misty patch; almost a fog. The church looked forlorn in the dusk. Even the gilded ship on top of the tower seemed to have lost its jauntiness.

'No such thing as ghosts.' Fats tried to sound as if he meant it.

'N-no,' said Toby. 'Except, they might come in dreams, I suppose. You know that dream I had when I first came here, about meeting the Warden down in the Wasteland, helping him make a garden there, and talking about rebuilding the church? Well, first I thought it was just a dream, and that I'd put the doc into it because I liked the look of him. Only I got to thinking, later, that there was more to it than that. I think it really was the Warden that I saw, and the doc looks like him because the doc is the Warden's grandson.'

'Self-hypnosis,' said Fats grandly, giving a quick glance out of the window to make sure. 'Me mum says it's stupid to believe in what you can't prove. You don't really think Skinny saw the Warden's ghost, do you?'

'I don't know. He was really frightened.'

'Stands to reason, if he had seen a ghost . . . not that

they exist, of course.'

'It doesn't make sense. There was nothing frightening about the Warden. He was more real, more friendly than a stranger.'

'Well, maybe it's like Skinny said; the old man doesn't like being disturbed. You can't blame him. I mean, who'd want Mike camping on his doorstep?'

Toby was silent. He didn't know which way up he was. It was a relief not to have to take more food to Skinny, but there were a lot of uneasy questions hanging around in his mind.

It began to drizzle. He'd promised to deliver leaflets for his mum tomorrow. If it rained, his shoes would leak. His mum was right; the church people would be bound to accept a good offer from a developer, and then the tower would be pulled down, and they'd dig up the Wasteland for foundations to build on . . . and they'd have lots of useful buildings without any heart.

'Depressing outlook, ain't it?' said Fats. 'So let's get on with this algebra. . .'

That night Toby woke with the feeling that someone had called his name. He sat up, listening. Was that something hitting his window? There it came again! Like a handful of gravel, perhaps.

There was no sound from the floor below, where his mum and Nikki slept. He'd drawn the thin curtains, but a dim light came through from the street lamps outside. Everything looked normal.

But it didn't feel normal. He listened so hard he felt his ears grow larger. A taxi went by in the distance. Silence.

It wasn't a peaceful, two o'clock in the morning and all's well, silence. It was a waiting, watchful silence. The sort you get between two bouts of angry shouting.

Toby got colder and colder. Fear seeped into the room from outside, from the Wasteland.

Toby knew where the fear was coming from, and he knew he had to look out of the window, to confirm or deny it. He didn't want to look. If he didn't look, he wouldn't know for sure.

He felt his chest grow tight, and began to wheeze. Reaching for the inhaler unstuck him. He whiffed in, and his breathing eased. Now was the time to dive under the bedclothes and go back to sleep. Except he couldn't. He had to look.

He inched up the right-hand corner of the curtain and peered out. A dirty grey mist hung over the shack and most of the Wasteland, but over by the church, by the side door, there was a light. It wasn't the pinprick light of a torch, nor yet the glow of a street light. It was a diffused light, with a greenish tone to it.

Toby felt as if he'd turned to stone. He told himself to move, and couldn't. He gripped the curtain so hard that the material hurt his fingers. The green light dimmed as a dark figure moved in front of it. A tall man stood there, wearing something loose, like a track suit . . . or an Air Raid Warden's uniform! He had an old tin helmet on his head. He looked straight up at Toby, and raised his right arm in a threatening gesture.

Toby felt his asthma take over. He must have blacked out, for when he opened his eyes again, he was huddled against the window, shivering. Mist swirled over the Wasteland, but the light and the figure had vanished.

Toby thought he was going to die. He couldn't breathe. His heart was going bang bang, and there was sweat on his face.

He groped for his inhaler till he could breathe more easily. He couldn't go back to sleep. He lay propped up on his pillows, trying not to be afraid . . . and not succeeding.

In the morning his mum took one look at him and screeched that she hadn't time to take him to the doc's and what did he mean by getting into such a state. Toby said he'd be all right and that he wanted to go to school. He certainly didn't want to stay at home in a room overlooking the ghost's territory.

His mum grumbled but Toby got his way and went to school, promising to call in on the doc's on his way home. His mum said they'd have to sign on with another doctor in future. Toby didn't want that. He really liked the doc. It was going to be embarrassing, going to see the doc, after what his mum had said and done.

The surgery was full and Toby had to wait a long time. Several times he thought of giving up and going home, but he told himself that was being cowardly, and in any case, he was so tired he couldn't make himself move.

'So what's up, Toby?' said the doc, when Toby dragged himself in. 'The usual? You look as if you've had a bad night.'

'Yes,' said Toby, and didn't know what else to say. The doc examined him, and asked how often he had to use the inhaler and all the usual questions doctors think are so important.

'You've been so much better all this summer,' said the doc. 'What's wrong? Is it what happened in church yesterday?'

Well, it was, and it wasn't. It was his mum quarrelling with the doc, and the Beard taking over, and Mike and Skinny and then . . . the awful thing he'd seen in the night. Toby hadn't the words to explain. He just looked at the doc, and the doc leaned forward and put his hands over both of Toby's. There was a look on the doc's face which told Toby that the doc really cared about him.

'Can't you stop it all going wrong, doc?' said Toby. 'Warn Mike off, and keep the church safe . . . and make up with Mum?'

'I wish I could, Toby. I have tried. I'll go on trying . . . but sometimes . . . it takes two, you know.'

Toby couldn't go on talking about his mum. It choked him, just to think of her quarrelling with the doc. So he ducked round that. He couldn't tell on Skinny, and he wasn't about to sign on for the funny farm by talking about ghosts, but he could talk about Mike.

'Couldn't you tell the police to move Mike off the site? Everyone knows he's planning something big and is going to take a holiday on the proceeds. Can't anyone stop him?'

'Is anybody pepared to go to the police and give evidence? No, I thought not.' The doc sighed, and made a note on his pad. 'The problem is that the Wasteland is private property, owned by the church, and the police have no right to search the shack or turn Mike off it. A friendly word, that's all they can give. It can't be for long, anyway. Mr Red has been given a contract to repair the broken hoardings around the site. After that, no-one will be able to get in, and the Wasteland will be safe.'

'But will it? With Mike taking over, it's a different place. Almost scary.' Toby tried to laugh, to show he personally wasn't scared.

'You feel it, too?' The doc looked into space. Then he shook himself back to normality. 'It will be all right, you'll see. Everything's undecided, that's all. And Mr Gaunt's still poorly. He won't let Mrs Gaunt out of his sight. If you've time, perhaps you would call round and offer to do some shopping for her. I'm arranging for a home help, but it takes time . . .'

He indicated that Toby should take his new prescription and leave.

In the doorway, Toby hesitated. 'I've been wondering. Who found Mr Gaunt after the accident?'

'Hm? Oh, Skinny popped in here with a message. He heard someone cry out when he was passing the church. Lucky, really. Mr Gaunt might have lain there for hours, otherwise.'

'And the keys?' said Toby with a feeling that he didn't really want to hear the answer.

'Handed in to my receptionist. Mrs Gaunt has them now . . . which reminds me . . .' and he made another note on his pad, '. . . "check keys" . . .'

'Something's wrong with the keys?' said Toby.

'Not sure. I'd better check, though. Now, my lad,

you'd best be on your way or your mother will be worrying.'

'Was there one key too many,' asked Toby, 'or one too few?'

The phone rang, and the doc turned to answer it. Toby waited a while, but the call went on and on, so he opened the door to leave. The doc covered the phone with his hand and said, 'Toby . . . one thing. Don't forget the rabbit and the fly.' He turned back to his caller, and said, 'Yes, yes, I've got that. I'll be round as soon as I've finished surgery.'

Toby went home. The flat was dark and empty. His mum had left him a note, saying she and Nikki were out delivering leaflets, but they'd be back soon. There was a stack of them on the table, waiting for him to cope with. But not tonight.

He went upstairs and looked out over the misty Wasteland. Mike was the intruder. Maybe the ghost was an intruder, too. Toby was the rabbit. Could the frog really do something about Mike and the ghost?

Fats helped Toby deliver some of the leaflets, on their way home from school. Toby's right shoe filled with water.

Fats said, 'Here, let me carry your bag. You look wore out.'

'I'm all right,' said Toby, feeling he could easily get angry with Fats. He wasn't made of paper, was he? He stopped on the corner of the Row. 'I've got to call in on the Gaunts, see if she wants any shopping. I promised the doc.'

Fats said, 'You'll catch your death. You wait till your mum hears. Straight out of the doc's and do-gooding all over the place.'

Toby grinned at a sour thought. 'Me mum wouldn't say that delivering her leaflets was do-gooding!'

Fats laughed, and hit Toby on the back as he knocked on the Gaunts' front door. The door shone with umpteen coats of paint. The brass – real brass – knocker and letter-box glittered with polish. The window to the right of the door winked as if the sun had come out; which it hadn't.

Mrs Gaunt let them in. She'd put sheets of newspaper along the hallway, so callers wouldn't trample the wet into her carpets.

'The doc said . . .' Toby began.

'. . . about time, too!' she said, reaching for her coat. 'What kept you? School's been out three quarters of an hour. I won't be long. He's asleep, but if he wakes, give him a cuppa and tell him I've gone to get something for his supper . . .'

She whisked out of the door, and slammed it in their faces.

Toby said, 'The doc must have called, and mentioned he'd asked me to pop round . . .'

'. . . and the old dear's got hold of the wrong end of the stick!'

'Well, we can't leave Mr Gaunt alone. We'll just have to wait till she gets back. She said she wouldn't be long.'

'If you believe that,' said Fats, 'you'll believe anything!'

Toby eased off his wet shoe. He tore off half a sheet of newspaper, and stuffed it into his shoe. It might blot up some of the wet. They took their school bags through into the kitchen, to make a start on their homework.

The kitchen was polished, too. Not a crumb in sight. But a tray had been left out, laid for Mr Gaunt's tea. They settled themselves down at the table and started on their maths, but within half an hour they heard Mr Gaunt calling for his wife. Toby went upstairs while Fats wrestled with the kettle on the gas stove.

Mr Gaunt's colour was a little better, but he didn't seem able to concentrate. No sooner had Toby explained where Mrs Gaunt had gone, than the old man was turning to the window, saying he thought he'd heard bells.

'Ice-cream bells?' said Fats, bringing up the tea. 'Can't hear any, meself.'

'Church bells, of course!' said Mr Gaunt, angrily.

Toby and Fats exchanged winks, but Mr Gaunt saw them and screeched, 'You think I'm deaf? You think I'm losing my marbles?'

'It's the mosque down the road, perhaps,' said Toby, trying to calm Mr Gaunt. 'You know, the Muslims call the faithful to prayer over their loudspeaker, umpteen times a day.'

'I know that! I'm not an idiot!' said Mr Gaunt. Then he relaxed against the pillows, and all of a sudden looked twenty years older. Fats gave him his tea, and made as if to pat the old man's hand, only stopping himself just in time. Fats had so many younger brothers that he sometimes got confused and played 'fathers' to the wrong person.

Mr Gaunt sighed, and closed his eyes. 'Church bells are the voice of God. We had bells once. Peter and Paul, they were called. I used to ring them, every Sunday. We weren't allowed to ring them in the war. They said it would help the enemy bombers to find us. Stupid. As if they didn't know where to find London, eh? But they stopped it, like they stopped a lot of good things. No bells. No lights. I thought, When peace comes, we'll put on all the lights in the church, and we'll ring the bells, and everyone will see we're still here . . . But it didn't work out that way.'

'The church was bombed just before the end of the war?'

'Smashed flat. The lead ran off the roof, the gutters, the pipes. It was all stolen before we could get in and reclaim it. The bells, too. But he paid for it, didn't he?'

'Who did?' asked Toby.

'Old Skinny, of course!'

6

Toby looked at Fats. Fats had his mouth open, gaping. Toby looked at Mr Gaunt, but the old man had dropped into the easy doze of convalescence. He had his mouth open, too.

The two boys tiptoed out and down the stairs.

Toby took his head in both hands, and shook it to see if it was still attached to his body. His brain definitely wasn't working properly.

'Now let's get this straight,' said Fats. 'He don't mean our Skinny. Our Skinny weren't born, then.'

'Nor was I.'

'Nor me, neither. It must be Skinny's father that he means.'

Toby said, 'Wait a mo. When did the war end? It was in the book, the diary I found in the tower. I wish I could find it.'

'Well, it's lost, so how do we find out?'

They both said together, 'History homework!'

The history books said the second World War ended in 1945, which gave them a date to work on. Skinny was the same age as them, eleven going on twelve.

'I seen our Skinny's dad,' said Fats, frowning hideously in an effort to remember. 'He used to live in the same flat Skinny and his mum and Mike are in, now. He used to drift around, sit in the sun, smoke ciggies, never shaved properly, got drunk a lot and then used to cry. Yuk. Just a little bloke. Me mum said he weren't all there. But nasty with it, if you know what I mean.'

'Nasty like Mike?'

'No, Mike's all there and he knows what he's doing when he's being nasty. His old man was . . . well . . .

he'd do something bad, like kicking a dog. A coupla secs after, he'd forget he'd done it, and try to give the dog a chip. Someone said he'd had a knock on the head, and lost what little sense he'd been born with. Skinny told me his dad had gone off when he was small, been away for yonks. Abroad, Skinny said. In jail, I thought. He was around till a coupla years ago. Died of drink, me mum said. I reckon he was sixtyish when he died, because me mum said he'd never get near his three score years and ten, and she was pleased when he didn't. Me mum won't have no drink in the house. Not even Christmastime.'

'You think Skinny's dad stole the bells and the lead from the church? How old would he have been at the end of the war? Fifteen, sixteen? Nar, it wouldn't have been him. Mr Gaunt's got it all wrong. Going ga-ga.'

'But the church hasn't got any bells.'

'The church people probably sold them, after the place was bombed.'

A key turned in the lock, and Mrs Gaunt came in, twisting up her mouth at the sight of Toby's wet shoes in her clean hall, and the mess they'd made with their homework on the kitchen table. She pointed out that Fats had forgotten to turn off the gas, and it was licking round the bottom of the empty kettle. The boys apologised, and scuffled their belongings together while she acted like they'd brought in the plague.

'We took Mr Gaunt up some tea, and he was all right, honest,' said Fats.

'Wanted to talk about the old days, the bells and that,' said Toby, wincing as he drew on his sopping shoe and tried to find somewhere to put the wodge of wet newspaper from inside it. Mrs Gaunt glared at him when he tried to put it in the sink drainer.

Toby said, trying to distract her, 'Mr Gaunt was telling us about old Skinny stealing the bells . . .'

'Now there never was no proof of that,' she said, tightening up her mouth again. 'I've told him, that's slander, and what's slander but bearing false witness! Just because Old Man Skinny was found dead at the wheel of a stolen lorry next morning, there's no proof he stole the lead and the bells. And you can put that wet paper in your pocket, my lad, and take it home with you. And next time you be here half four sharp, so's I can get my shopping done before they're sold out of bread.'

'Yes, Mrs Gaunt.'

'Of course, Mrs Gaunt.'

The two boys backed out of the house into the drizzle, and ran for Toby's house. It was a horrid dark afternoon. Lights were already on in the shops and flats around. As they passed the Wasteland they saw a blue flickering light coming from the shack. For a moment Toby felt frightened. What devilry was Mike up to now? Then he realised that Mike had fixed himself up with a portable telly.

The two boys let themselves into Toby's place and went upstairs to the kitchen, where Toby shed his shoes and got them both a drink of Coke. They hadn't liked to help themselves even to a cup of tea at the Gaunts'.

'Funny,' said Fats, 'how some people think they're so holy, but don't even offer us a drink of squash.'

'. . . and make us feel we've done them an injury by trying to help them.'

'Mr Gaunt's not like that. He'd have given us a cuppa if he'd been in her shoes.'

'Wonder how he likes being married to old Sour-face.'

'Got used to her, I suppose. She's a good cook, they say.'

Toby up-ended the biscuit tin, which was empty except for broken bits. They ate the broken bits, licked their fingers and mopped up the crumbs.

'If only we could get hold of that diary,' mourned Toby. 'I never read it all through. I'm sure it would help.'

'You want to get back into the tower to look for it?

I'll come with you, if you like. Stand guard. See if Skinny's all right.'

Toby choked on a crumb and gulped Coke. He hadn't told anyone about the ghost, but he couldn't get it out of his mind. He hadn't been able to sleep properly last night, and he didn't think he'd do any better tonight. How could he sleep, knowing the ghost was out there in the Wasteland, looking up at his window!

Toby remembered what the doc had said. He'd been trying to put his advice into action all day, but every time he'd nerved himself up to start telling Fats about it, something had happened.

Fats said, 'Where's your mum and Nikki?'

'Doing a big food shop. Mum told me not to go anywhere near the church, nor the Wasteland . . . but, Fats!'

'Well,' said Fats, 'Mike'll soon be gone and then everything will be all right again.'

'I'm not so sure. Fats. . .'

'Bound to be. Then Skinny can come out of hiding, and . . . I wonder what he thinks of Mike sitting up there, almost over his head, watching telly while . . .'

'Fats! I got something to tell you.'

'No need to shout. I'm here, ain't I?'

'It's about the Wasteland and the tower. I saw the ghost, too. A coupla nights ago I woke up and saw . . .'

Toby told Fats everything. Fats looked out of the window, even though the kitchen looked out over the backs of houses and not over the Wasteland.

'. . . and I saw it again last night, though I didn't want to look. But somehow I just had to.'

'You think that's what Skinny saw?'

'I suppose so,' said Toby. 'But it's all wrong, Fats. The Warden wouldn't frighten anyone.'

'But it was the same chap?'

'Yes. No. I don't know. I suppose it could have been. Fats, don't you see what this means? Mike may leave, but suppose the ghost stays? Will we ever be able to go into the tower again?'

'It's not just a tower. It's a church. No-one can keep us out of a church.'

'But don't you see, it's not a church at the moment, even though the doc's taken a coupla services there. It's neither one thing nor the other. Like the Wasteland. Mike's taken over the Wasteland and turned it bad, and I think . . .'

'. . . he's taken over the church and turned that bad, too?'

'No. Of course he couldn't do that. I don't know what I mean, Fats. I'm so mixed up, I can't think straight.'

'Well, there's nothing we can do about it, is there? Let the grown-ups sort it out.'

Toby said, 'You haven't thought it through, Fats. If there's a ghost in the church and he doesn't like intruders, then what about poor old Skinny? He must be scared out of his mind. We know he's scared. We promised to help him, but what have we done? Let him stay on there, getting more and more scared. I think we ought to try to get him out of there. He could stay with you till Mike goes, couldn't he? Or I could smuggle him up to my bedroom and he could hide in the big cupboard if Mum came up.'

'But Toby, we couldn't!'

'Yes, we could. Oh, I'm scared, too. I'm scared rigid. I'll have asthma attacks every minute till we get him out. But if we do it right away, before it gets properly dark, then the ghost won't be around. Mike and his lot are watching the telly. We could sneak in through the broken hoarding and get in the secret way, pull Skinny out, and be back here before Mum and Nikki return. Are you on, or do I have to do it by myself?'

Fats couldn't go pale, but his skin took on an ashen tinge. He gulped a bit, then said, 'All right. If you can take it, so can I. One thing; I don't think I can crawl through that little window. You'll have to go in by yourself while I stand guard.'

Toby got his trainers and pulled on an old cagoule. It wasn't much past six, but you'd have thought it was mid-winter, the sky was so dark with rain. The shack shone with a livid blue light as they passed it, and from inside came the acrid smell of baked beans burning.

They slipped through the broken hoarding, and pressing close to the flattened, dripping shrubs and broken weeds, made their way into the sheltered corner by the side door.

Toby pointed to a clear space by the wall. 'That's where the ghost stood.'

Fats gave the spot a wide berth. He wrenched out the plywood over the window frame, and helped Toby slide inside the tower. It was darker and colder than ever inside. Toby wished he'd remembered the torch, and then was glad he hadn't because Mike might see the glow and come to investigate.

There was no sound from below. Toby fumbled his way down the stairs until he came to the grille. He could feel his heart going bang, bang, and his chest begin to squeeze tight. He'd forgotten to bring his inhaler. He felt along the bars till he came to the latch and pressed down on it to open the grille. It wouldn't shift.

He pressed the latch again, and pushed, putting his weight behind it.

It still wouldn't shift.

Someone had locked the grille with Skinny inside!

Toby panicked. He clutched the uprights of the grille and shook them. 'Skinny!' he yelled in a hoarse whisper. 'Skinny, are you there? Are you all right?'

He heard someone come down the stairs behind him, and assumed it was Fats.

'Help me, Fats! Someone's locked Skinny in and . . .'

'It's not Fats,' said a well-known and very unwelcome voice. 'It's me!'

7

Toby gave a silent shriek. 'Nikki! How could you!'

A pale yellow light glowed around him from Nikki's pocket torch. She played it over the grille.

'Did you think I was a ghost, or something?' she said. 'I spotted Fats lurking ouside, when Mum and I were on our way back from the shops. She was cross that you weren't home yet and I said I'd seen you talking on the corner with Fats and I'd come and get you. I didn't tell her you were probably in the church, or she'd have thrown a wobbler.'

Toby gulped. 'Keep your voice down, for heavens' sake!'

'Why? Fats can't hear. I got right up behind him and said "Woo!" He jumped into the air and came down the other side of Greenwich, I shouldn't wonder! So then I saw the cover was off the window, and sussed you were down here. What I want to know is, why?'

'Hush! They'll hear you . . .'

'Who?' said Nikki, raising rather than lowering her voice.

A pale face and hands appeared on the other side of the grille, and this time both Nikki and Toby jumped.

'Hey!' whispered Skinny, 'You two want to get me in trouble?'

'Skinny,' said Nikki. 'What you doing here?'

'Skinny,' said Toby. 'I came to get you out. It's not safe for you to stay . . .'

'I'm safe enough,' said Skinny, 'but if Mike catches you, I wouldn't give much for your chances. Cut and run while you can!'

'Why should Mike . . .' started Nikki, but Toby cut

her short.

'Nikki, I'll tell you later. Just for now, shut up, will you? Listen Skinny, I saw the ghost, too. It's not safe for you to stay, I'll hide you somewhere . . .'

'Ghost?' said Nikki, and burst into noisy laughter, quickly hushed by the two boys.

'Shut it!' said Skinny, in a strangled shriek. He glanced over his shoulder, looking really scared. Nikki quietened down. 'Listen, I'm safe enough down here. The ghost said so. He knows I won't bother him none. A coupla days, that's all. I've got food, and me radio and some comics. I'm all right, so long as you lot keep away. Tell the others, OK? Just keep them away till Mike's finished . . .'

'Finished what?' said Toby.

'I mean, till he's gone!' Skinny corrected himself.

'But you've been locked in!

'Eh? Er . . . me mum did that. To keep me safe.'

'What? Why should she do that?'

'Well, er, she thought it best . . . keep me out of Mike's way . . . you know. It's all right, honest. but it wouldn't be all right if Mike caught you down here. Just go, will you? If he hears you . . .'

Skinny faded back into the crypt. One moment he was there, palely hovering, and the next he was gone, and there was silence.

'Sounds odd to me,' said Nikki, but she lowered her voice.

'I don't like leaving him,' whispered Toby, but all the same he started back up the steps with Nikki. They waited at the top and listened, but nothing stirred except drops of rain from the sodden bushes above. They inched out into the open, jammed the board back over the window, and ran for it.

Fats was lurking in the doorway of the doc's surgery, waiting for them. He gave Nikki a filthy look. It took a lot to get Fats going, but she'd succeeded. He said, 'I knew it was you, all along. I'd have come back, but

Mike's mate Ricky came outa the shack, and saw me run off. Did he see you?'

'No, no-one saw us come out. Skinny won't budge. Anyway, we can't get him out now. The grille's locked. Skinny says his mum locked him in, though I don't know how she could have got hold of the key.'

Fats arranged to see them later, and went off home. Toby and Nikki went up to the flat.

Kate Webb was on the phone, twisting a strand of hair round her finger, and laughing. She was talking to Jeff, of course. She'd left all the groceries and meat on the table in the kitchen, so Toby and Nikki put things away while Toby told Nikki what had been happening. Nikki smirked when he told her about the ghost, but she didn't laugh, for which he was grateful.

'Funny peculiar,' said Nikki, pulling at and twisting a lock of hair, just like her mum. 'I've been talking to my friend Jan about this. Everyone's talking about the Wasteland and what's going to happen to it. And if they're not talking about the Wasteland, they're wondering what Mike's up to. Even Mum and Jeff wonder what he's up to. The thing is, we need the Wasteland, and the church building, and the crypt. Mum and Jeff have got plans for it, and so have I and my friends. That land isn't used by anyone, so . . .'

'It belongs to the church people . . .'

'. . . if they don't use it, they shouldn't be allowed to keep it. Mum says the council should buy it off them, and then we could have everything we want; a community centre with ballet classes and Brownies and discos and proper play equipment for holidays.'

'Everything *you* want, you mean,' said Toby. 'I bet Mum didn't put ballet classes on her list! Anyway, it's a church and churches are for praying in, and not for play!'

'They can be for both,' said a man's voice, behind them. The doc came in, smiling. 'You two shot upstairs in such a hurry you forgot to close the front door. Toby, are you all right? You're limping.'

Toby curled his wet foot round behind his other leg as his mum hove into sight. She didn't look pleased to see the doc, and reached for her ciggies.

'I just dropped in to say hello,' said the doc, with one of his best smiles. It went down like a ton of bricks.

'Oh. Nice of you,' she said, refusing to smile back.

He stopped smiling. 'I've arranged a meeting for next Friday night at the surgery, after hours. I've got someone coming down from Church House to talk to us. He wants to hear all our views, and give us theirs. Will you be able to make it?'

'Shouldn't think so,' she said, giving him a slitty-eyed look over her cigarette smoke. 'Got an important meeting myself, that night.'

'Oh. Well. Perhaps you could send a representative?'

'Perhaps you should have asked me if it was convenient before you arranged your meeting.'

'You knew I was trying to get everyone together . . .'

'I can't think why you bother, since we all know the site is being sold to a developer.'

'We know nothing of the kind!'

'The best we can hope for,' she said, 'is to make so much of a stink, to give you lot so much bad publicity, that you include a community hall in your rebuilding plans. I'll settle for that, and so will all those who really care for the people here.'

The doc went red and did a bit of deep breathing. He said, 'You seem determined to quarrel, but I won't give you the satisfaction. Mrs Webb, I would like your permission to look at Toby's foot. He's limping.'

'It's nothing!' said Toby, hastily. 'Just my shoe leaks.'

Now it was his mum's turn to go red. 'Why didn't you tell me, Toby! I've just done this big food shop, and put a downpayment on a new tracksuit for Nikki. Why didn't you tell me you needed new shoes?'

'But you already knew, Mum,' said Nikki, with a round-eyed, innocent look.

The doc choked. Toby couldn't decide whether he was angry, or trying not to laugh. One look at his mum's face told him she wasn't laughing, though. She was livid with him, and with the doc, and probably with herself as well.

Toby thought he'd better try to save the situation if he could, so he said, 'Could I go to the meeting as your representative, Mum?'

'No,' said his mum, at the same time as the doc said, 'Sure!'

They did another bit of glaring at one another, and then the doc said, 'May I make a suggestion? There's a sale on at the shoe shop on the corner. I'm going that way now. Suppose I take Toby in and get him a pair of shoes, and you pay me back at the end of the month.'

'I . . .' his mum didn't know what to say. Nikki was grinning. Toby could almost see the words in a balloon over her head, 'Jeff bought *me* a pair, and I didn't even need them!'

Kate said, 'Certainly not! I wouldn't dream of allowing you to buy things for my children. I'll . . . I'll take Nikki's tracksuit back, get a refund, and get Toby some new shoes in the sale.'

Nikki stopped grinning and scowled, but everyone else saw this was the only possible answer to the problem.

Nikki did a bit of ringing around, and got her special mates Jan and Clare to come round after supper. Nikki told their mum that they had to work on some homework together, but really it was to have a committee meeting about the Wasteland. Fats and Red also came round, so there were six of them all up in Toby's room while Kate had an entirely different sort of committee meeting downstairs with her politically-inclined friends.

Fats brought a plastic bag with him. He pulled Toby aside and said, out of the corner of his mouth, 'I grow out of shoes faster than me brothers grow into them, so we gotta whole stack of them saved, sitting doing nothing in the cupboard. I put a coupla pairs in this bag; see if any fit. If they do, you can let me have them back when you get new ones. Only just don't tell me mum, right?'

Toby felt all choked about that. Fats hit him on the back, and said out loud to the others, 'So what we going to do about all this, then?'

Jan and Clare were a couple of girls who followed Nikki around. One was very tall and thin, and the other was small and plump, so they were usually known as The Long and The Short Of It. They were nice kids, but Toby didn't expect bright ideas from them, because they were definitely Indians and not Chiefs.

Red said, 'Well, one thing's for certain; we gotta do something!'

'Such as?' said Fats, electing himself chairman of the meeting.

'Well . . . tell someone, I suppose,' said Red, his face going as red as his hair at being singled out for attention.

'But you can't do anything about ghosts, can you?' said the tall, earnest Clare. 'I mean . . . ghosts are ghosts.'

'My aunt saw a ghost once,' said Jan, the plump one.

'Not now, Jan,' said Nikki, in world-weary fashion.

'But she did!' insisted Jan.

'What did she do about it, then?' said Toby.

'Well . . . nothing,' said Jan. 'I mean, you can't, can you?'

'I think you can,' said Fats. 'I think church people know how. They fight evil with good words, or something.'

'Lights and bells,' said Toby, with a sigh. 'That's what Mr Gaunt said. That the evil war attacked everything good in the church, that the evil stopped our having lights, and silenced the bells . . .'

'What's that got to do with it?' demanded Nikki. 'I for one don't believe in ghosts.'

'But Toby saw the Warden in a dream when he first came here . . .'

'OK, he had a funny dream. But he says he was awake

when he saw the ghost last night and the night before. And he says the ghost wasn't the same one.'

'I said I wasn't sure,' protested Toby. 'I agree that dreams are one thing, and ghosts another. In my dream the Warden wasn't frightening. He was lovely. But what I saw the other night . . .'

'I'd love to see a real ghost!' said Jan, all envious.

'You wouldn't, really,' said Nikki, crushing her. 'You'd be scared, probably, and run away.'

'I thought you said you didn't believe in ghosts, Nikki.'

'Well, I don't. But if there were ghosts, I don't think they'd be like the one Toby and Skinny saw. You lot just aren't thinking straight. One: Mike moves onto the Wasteland for reasons unknown but probably he's up to no good as usual. Two: he warns everyone off the Wasteland. Three: Skinny hides out from Mike under the Wasteland, and four: he sees a ghost who tells him to keep away . . . and then Toby sees it, too. So what does all that add up to?'

Fats said, 'You mean the ghost is helping Mike to keep people away from the Wasteland? But that means . . .'

'That it's not a real ghost!' said Nikki, triumphantly. 'And I vote we set up a ghost watch, and prove it!'

8

Toby was not happy. He'd kept quiet during their committee meeting. It wasn't that he was against doing something about Mike or the ghost. He just didn't feel they were going the right way about it.

He kept his misgivings to himself. Maybe it would be all right. Nikki was so much braver than he was, and she had a head start on him in that she wouldn't let herself believe in ghosts. Jan and Clare thought Nikki was wonderful, and so did Red. Fats was frowning and not saying much, but he didn't do anything to stop Nikki going ahead.

It was agreed that Nikki should change bedrooms with Toby for the night, to keep a lookout for the ghost. Nikki's room looked out over the street at the back, and up towards the flats, but it didn't have a window onto the Wasteland. They decided not to tell their mum, in case she raised objections. Anyway, she was still in her own committee meeting.

The girls helped Nikki take her things upstairs, with a lot of giggling. Toby collected his Bible and his pyjamas and wished her luck. Their mum came out of her meeting to say it was time Toby and Nikki were in bed, so the others went home, and the flat was soon as quiet as . . . as quiet as the grave. Toby didn't like the thought of it being as quiet as the grave, but that was the thought that kept coming into his head.

He got into Nikki's bed and read a bit of the Bible before he turned off his light and tried to sleep. He didn't like Nikki's room much, and her bed was too soft. He heard his mother's committee friends leave, making a lot of noise. He wondered how Nikki was getting on upstairs. Perhaps she'd fall asleep quickly, as she usually did, and not see the ghost at all.

Toby felt bad about letting her take his room. It made him out to be a coward, to let a girl take his place.

He couldn't get comfortable in the bed. First he was too hot, and then he was too cold. At last he convinced himself that nothing was going to happen, and fell asleep.

But not for long!

He was woken by a wailing noise, which got louder and louder, and turned into Nikki screaming her head off as she ran down the stairs from his room.

She didn't try his door, but blundered into their mum's bedroom. She came straight out again, because Kate wasn't there.

'Whatever's the matter!' cried their mum, crashing out of the sitting-room. 'Why, Nikki! I'm here, darling! Whatever's wrong?'

Toby shot upright in Nikki's bed, and began to shiver. He knew what was wrong. Nikki had seen the ghost!

Nikki went on screaming, but the screams were muffled now, as her mum held her tight.

'She's had a bad dream, poor kid!' said Kate. 'There, there, now. There's nothing to worry about. You're quite safe now!'

'What a fuss over a bad dream!' This was a man's voice. Jeff's voice, thought Toby. Jeff must have stayed on for a quiet chat after the end of the committee meeting, and he wasn't pleased to be interrupted by a screaming girl.

'She can't help it!' said their mum. 'There now, little one! Do you want a drink of water?'

'Pull yourself together, girl!' said Jeff, loudly. 'What a fuss about nothing!'

Toby thought the doc would have managed much better. With a bit of luck, their mum might think so, too.

'Don't talk to her like that!' said Kate. 'Come along, darling. Come into the kitchen, and I'll make you a hot drink. You can spend the rest of the night in my bed, if you like. Jeff, can you see yourself out?'

'Surely the child can manage. You have to be firm with children, or they take advantage of . . .'

'Please, Jeff,' said their mum, sounding cross and tired. 'Can't you see the child's upset?'

Nikki's screams had moderated to heavy sobs. Toby heard the front door bang as Jeff retreated, and then he heard the door of the kitchen close as Nikki was taken off for a cuddle and a drink.

Toby took his Bible and tiptoed back up to his own room.

The curtain had been drawn back, and the room was dimly lit by the lamps in the street outside. Nothing moved down in the Wasteland. No ghost, no green light. Nothing.

A faint glow came from the shack. Rumour had it that Mike and his friends took turns to sleep in the shack at night. Toby wondered why the ghost didn't frighten them. He stood there getting cold, wondering about all sorts of things.

Toby thought that the one thing they hadn't done in their committee meeting that evening was to ask Jesus to guide and help them. Perhaps that was why Fats had been quiet that evening, too. Fats and he had both known better than to engage the enemy without proper preparation, but they'd let Nikki overrule them. Now Nikki had been humbled, and they had to think again.

The words of a man who knew all about fear came into Toby's mind: David, the psalmist, had fought Goliath and been soldier and fugitive before he became king of Israel. Toby sank to his knees beside the bed and closed his eyes.

'. . . where will my help come from? My help will come from the Lord, who made heaven and earth . . . The Lord will guard you; he is by your side to protect you. The sun will not hurt you during the day, nor the moon during the night. The Lord will protect you from all danger; he will keep you safe . . . now and for ever.'

He felt a new kind of strength flood into him, and through him out into the room. He felt safe and, incredibly, full of joy.

He looked out over the Wasteland, and it was like looking with new eyes. Terror had fled from it, and he could imagine it was almost like it had been in the old days, or as it had been in his dream, when he'd helped the Warden make a garden there.

'Guide us, Lord,' Toby prayed. 'We've been so stupid, not bringing this problem to you before. If we'd asked you to help us from the beginning, we wouldn't have got ourselves into this mess. Tell us what to do. Please help poor Skinny, and Mr Gaunt . . . and the doc and our mum . . . and Nikki. Amen.'

He went to pull the curtain, and as he did so, something caught his eye . . . some movement by the church, near the secret entrance, where the ghost had appeared. But it wasn't the ghost. It wasn't the green light, either. It was . . . puzzling. He could have sworn that for a flicker of an eyelash, he'd seen a man carrying a body away on his back.

It didn't make sense.

He asked himself if he was frightened, and found that he wasn't. He lay down in bed, drew the duvet over him, and went straight off to sleep. In the morning, he'd know what to do.

Nikki was pale and quiet next morning. Luckily it was Saturday, and they didn't need to go to school. She stayed in bed – in her mother's bed – while Toby went with their mum to return the tracksuit and get him a pair of shoes. He'd tried on the ones Fats had brought, but they were like boats on his feet. It made him feel warm all over, when he thought of Fats bringing him the shoes, and also of the doc offering to buy him a pair. But it was only right and proper that they bought the shoes themselves, if they could.

When Toby got back, he went to see Nikki, who was

sitting up in bed, looking uncharacteristically fragile.

Toby said, 'Sorry about the tracksuit, Nikki.'

' 'Salright,' said Nikki. 'I can manage with my old one for a bit.' She lowered her eyes. 'Sorry about last night. I didn't believe you'd really seen anything. I thought you'd just had a bad dream. I didn't think anything could frighten me like that. At least you didn't scream and run!'

'The ghost *is* frightening. But Nikki, I've worked out where we went wrong. We can't cope with this kind of thing by ourselves. We need help.'

'Nobody would believe us.'

'God would. He does. We ought to have asked him to guide us from the beginning.'

'Yar. What can he do that we can't?'

'Plenty,' said Toby, still feeling the unusual certainty that had come to him last night. 'He can take away our fear, and help us think straight. You were right and there is a mystery. Something very peculiar is going on in the Wasteland, and it's up to us to find out what it is.'

'Now look, I'm not going ghost-hunting again!'

'Nobody asked you,' said Toby.

'So what are we supposed to do? You tell me that, if you're so clever!'

'I'm not sure yet, but I think we start by putting our fear aside and looking at the facts. I want to search the Wasteland properly, and I'd also like a look in Mike's shack, if we can . . .'

'We've been forbidden. If you're so holy, how come you want us to do something we've been forbidden to do?'

'I don't know that yet, either. I think that if we go on praying about it, we'll find out exactly what we're supposed to do.'

'You know I don't believe in your God.'

'That's your loss,' said Toby, secure in his new-found serenity. 'It won't stop me praying.'

'Yar, yar, yar!' said Nikki. She dived under the duvet and pulled it over her head to show that as far as she was concerned, the conversation was over.

Kate yelled to Toby that someone was banging on the front door, so he went down to find the doc there, with Fats, Red and Nikki's friends in the background. They were all fidgeting, wanting to know how Nikki had got on, but they wouldn't ask in front of the doc.

The doc looked down at Toby's feet, and grinned when he saw the new shoes. He said, 'I won't bother your mum today, since I expect she's busy. I just wanted to tell you that Mr Red has got the order through to start repairing the hoarding around the Wasteland. Mrs Gaunt has given him the keys but he'll be glad to have you lot around, to see Mike and his friends don't pinch anything while his back's turned. The church people are sending someone down to tell Mike to move on, and if he doesn't, they'll start the law moving. OK?'

'You mean it's all right for us to go into the Wasteland now?' said Toby, hardly daring to believe that his prayer for guidance had been answered so quickly. 'And into the tower, too?'

'Yes, of course. Did I hear you'd left your binoculars and diary in the tower? Well, go get them!'

'How about that!' said Toby. 'Let's get Nikki, and go, go, go!'

9

'It's an odd thing,' said Fats, 'but I always feel good coming up here.' They climbed the last few steps and entered the Lookout room in the tower.

'Ouch!' said Toby.

Fats drew in his breath. The baddies had been here, and set their mark on the place. Even up in the tower itself.

Some time ago Fats had used his spray can to create a large cross on the plastered wall. He'd said a church needed a cross, and even if this wasn't an active church, they needed to be reminded of what it was meant to be.

Someone had brought another spray can up here, and scrawled ugly words over the cross and the wall.

Fats went a strange, ashen colour. He turned round and was heading back down the stairs when Toby caught his arm and asked where he was going.

'Out. It's all spoiled.'

'Don't be daft. It'll wash off. We'll wash it off.'

'That stuff doesn't wash off. I oughta know. I done enough of it. You gotta paint over it.'

'Then we paint over it. We ask Mr Red if he's got some paint, and we get down to it.'

'Don't nothing ever get you down? I feel sick!'

Fats threw himself onto the bare-springed bed that the Warden had used during the war.

'It's like this,' said Toby, 'They're trying everything they know to spoil things for us. If we let them drive us away, then they've won.'

Fats muttered, 'I suppose I deserve this. I done enough spraying myself. I didn't know it could make you feel sick to your stomach.'

Toby looked for his binoculars, and found them in their case, tucked behind the bed. He pounced on them, grinning. Then he dropped them again.

He said, ' "Someone's been sitting in my chair." '

'What's up? They're not broken, are they?'

'Someone else has been using them. I can tell. They've been adjusted wrong.'

'Well, at least you can use them without feeling sick.'

Toby went on poking around. 'The diary's not here. I wish we could find it.'

'Maybe Skinny took it to read. We oughta go down and say hello to him.' Neither of them made a move. It was unthinkable to leave this bright, airy room to go down into the dungeon-like crypt.

Fats continued, 'I suppose his mum's still got the key. I wonder what he thinks of us invading the place today . . .'

Toby focused the binoculars on the Wasteland below. Nikki, Jan and Clare were being helpful to Mr Red and his workman. They were holding things, and fetching and carrying and getting underfoot. They weren't going anywhere near the church, even though Mr Red had opened it up for them, and said they could go in. They were avoiding the corner where the ghost had stood, too. The only place they couldn't go was the crypt, because the key to the grille had gone missing.

'What's Mike doing?' said Fats. 'Has he come back yet?'

'That's mystery of the week, isn't it? What's Mike up to? No, he hasn't come back. There's just Ricky sitting in the door of the shack, smoking and drinking beer. You can see right in, today. Just one camp bed, one chair, that's all. No telly, no radio, no cooking gear.'

'Looks like they're prepared to move out today, then.'

'Mm. Fats, you realise why we got nowhere till now? We didn't go at it right, did we?'

'You mean we didn't pray about it? I did try, once or twice. But somehow I couldn't concentrate.'

'I reckon it was because we were afraid, or just plain selfish. Or just didn't ask the right way. We asked for what *we* wanted, not what *he* wanted.'

Toby lowered the binoculars and looked up at the pale blue sky above. He liked to pray looking up at the sky. He didn't hold with praying in front of crosses and pictures and stuff. He knew it helped some people, but it didn't help him. He prayed for a bit, and when he stopped, he could feel the difference in the room. It was all clean and bright inside, just as if it had been freshly painted over, and even if the bad words were still on the wall, they didn't trouble him so much now. He looked at Fats. Fats had his eyes closed, and Toby realised that Fats was praying, too. Jesus had said that where two or more were gathered together in his name, he would be there, too. And it was true; two people praying together didn't half get a good effect!

He looked back out over the Wasteland, leaning on the window-sill. Soon they'd have to go down and relieve Nikki and Co. And have a word with Skinny. But in the meantime . . .

'What's up, eh?' said Fats.

'I've been thinking?'

'So what have you thunked?'

'The key. Mr Gaunt said he'd been pushed down the stairs. We didn't take much notice; silly old man's past it, we said. Mixed up in his mind, we said. But suppose he really was pushed! Suppose it was Mike who done it, to get the bunch of keys off Mr Gaunt. We know something's wrong with the keys that Mrs Gaunt's been looking after, and that Mr Red's got now. The doc was going to look into it. But I daresay he forgot. He's so busy. Now we know the key to the grille is missing . . .'

'But Skinny said it was his mum locked him in.'

'I know, but . . . it doesn't make sense. Skinny wouldn't knock Mr Gaunt down the stairs, and neither would his mum. The only reason anyone would want to do that, would be to get hold of the keys. And it's Mike who's been warning us off the place, not his mum.'

'So what are you getting at?'

'I don't know,' said Toby, unhappily. 'I can't think straight. Fats, will you come down to the crypt with me? I want to talk to Skinny, but first I want to suss the place out, so let's go down without making any noise, OK?' They took the binoculars and crept down the stairs. It gold colder and nastier as they went down. The entrance to the crypt was scarily dark, and the grille still locked. The boys tried to peer in: there was nothing but blackness to be seen. Toby sniffed, and gestured to Fats to do the same. Fats shrugged. He would have spoken, but Toby gestured to him to keep quiet. They stood there for what seemed to Fats to be a long, long time. He couldn't hear anything much. Just the usual street noises, faintly. Pipes knocking. Scratching sounds, like mice. The usual.

Toby turned back up the last few stairs and came down them, making a lot of noise. He banged on the grille, and shouted 'Skinny!'

Nothing happened. Everything went on as before. Skinny didn't come to the grille and no lights appeared in the crypt. The silence was unbearable. You couldn't even hear the mice scratching, now. Toby shouted a couple of times, and then gestured to Fats to follow him up the stairs.

Once they were in the open air Fats said, 'So what was all that about? He's gone walkabout, I suppose. Or scarpered, knowing that Mike's not around.'

'Odd, don't you think? I think he was still there, all right. Or someone was. I thought I could hear someone working down there at first, and smell something cooking, but after we made a noise, it stopped.'

'You're imagining things!'

'I don't think so. Suppose someone's put a black rug or curtain just inside the passage that leads to the rooms in the crypt. I've been wondering how Skinny could appear out of nowhere, and disappear so quickly, without showing a light. When we first visited him in the crypt, we could see the glow of his light, and hear his radio. But not lately. I think he's been blacked out, like they did in the war.'

'You mean, he's been taking precautions against Mike's hearing him or seeing his light? Well, bully for him.'

'I don't think Skinny would have made such a good job of it.'

Fats shrugged. 'OK, so his mum helped him. Makes sense.'

'Now come on! You heard the noises, at first!'

'The usual, mice and that.'

'Didn't you hear the tapping noise? Like a chisel on stone?' Fats burst out laughing. 'You and your ghosts! You'll be saying they're mining for gold under the church, next!'

Toby coloured up, but didn't reply.

'So what are you looking for now?' said Fats, as Toby began to look along the outside wall of the church.

'Clues,' said Toby. 'I'm Hawkeye, the Sherlock Holmes of Paradise Row, remember?'

'OK, Hawkeye. And I'm Dr Watson. So what're you looking for now? The ghost's footprints?'

'Yes,' said Toby. 'You can see there's been a lot of men walking around here. The ground's still wet, and shows footprints nicely. Trainers. Mike and his lot all wear trainers, don't they?'

'Ghosts don't leave footsteps. So Mike and his pals have been round here. Why not? They've taken the place over, haven't they?'

'Sure. They've been in the tower; we know that because of the graffiti, and the binoculars being altered. They'd leave their footprints, walking to and from the shack. Why not? But why would they have trodden around in this corner? It's not on their direct route. It's just a tucked-away little corner. You wouldn't think anyone would need to come and stand here, would you?

Unless they had business here . . . like setting up a "ghost" figure to frighten us off.'

Fats gaped at Toby, and then inspected the ground. It was quite true, what Toby said. You had to take two long steps off the path, to get to that corner. Standing there, you had a good view of Toby's window, but were screened from anyone passing by in the street.

The ground was badly churned up, all around a stake which had been driven deep into the ground, and stood maybe as high as Fats.

'That stake came from the hoarding, originally,' said Fats. 'So why has it been set up here?'

'To support the fake ghost, perhaps? If they tied a sort of scarecrow figure to the stake, and pulled the arms around with string, or propped them up with wire . . .'

'How about the green light?'

'Skinny had a battery-operated lamp. If you put a piece of thin green material over it, you'd get that sort of effect.'

'So where is Skinny? Toby, this is a lot more serious than we thought! We've got to find him! Suppose Mike's found him, and captured him, and got him locked up somewhere . . . Toby, we ought to go to the police!'

'And tell them we saw a ghost? OK, you can do that, if you like, but what I think is that we'd better find Skinny first, and tell the police after, when we've found out what Mike is really up to.'

'And how do we do that?'

'Get the others, and we'll have a Council of War. I've got a plan!'

10

'What is it, Toby?' said Nikki and Co., abandoning their care of Mr Red to join Toby and Fats. Red came, too. They all looked with careful disinterest at the area where Toby and his sister had seen the 'ghost'. It didn't look threatening in daylight, but it was still the Scene of the Horror Movie, as far as they were concerned.

'Listen,' said Toby, 'I haven't got it all worked out yet, but we gotta do something, and we gotta do it quick. Mike and his pals are moving out tonight, and I'm pretty sure they're finished – or almost finished – here.'

'What have they been up to, then?'

'I'm not entirely sure,' said Toby, hesitating.

'If you know, you ought to tell us.'

'Yes, well . . . I'm only guessing. If I could find the diary, I bet it would tell us whether I was right or wrong, but that's all part of it, isn't it? That, the new padlock on the side door and the key to the grille going missing. I think Mike hasn't left the site. I think he and Lewis are still here, working away at something down in the crypt.'

'Garn!'

'He's lost his marbles!'

'As loopy as old Mr Gaunt!'

'Now come on!' said Fats. 'Toby usually makes sense, doesn't he? It was he who thought up the plan to stop Mike mugging everyone he liked, back in the summer. I vote we listen to him.'

'OK,' said Jan, 'but not if it involves the ghost!'

'There is no ghost,' said Toby.

'Come on, I saw it!' said Nikki, turning pale.

'What you saw was a man-sized dummy, a scarecrow,

got up specially to frighten us. Mike knows we're the only ones likely to use the site now the adventure playground's finished. He tried to frighten us off with threats, and then he made sure, by inventing the "ghost". He tied it to this stake here, and he got it to wave its right arm around, and we got the message, didn't we?'

Nikki still looked dubious. 'But it was real! I saw it!'

'You saw a dummy figure, in a green light. You knew I'd seen it and thought it was a ghost. You knew Skinny had seen it, and been frightened. Come to think of it, if Skinny hadn't told us about it in the first place, maybe we wouldn't have been so ready to believe it was a ghost!'

'Yes, but . . .'

'So why does Mike want us off the place?'

'Well . . .' said Toby, 'It may sound daft, but I think he's got wind of something that's hidden down below in the crypt. It can't be that easy to get at, or he could just have walked in and taken it. It's hidden so well that it's taken him all this week to find it, so I don't think it's the proceeds from his own muggings and burglings.'

'Buried treasure?' said Red, hopefully.

'I think it is buried, yes. Or maybe bricked up behind one of the walls down in the crypt. I think the diary might have helped us there. I noticed there was a map of the crypt at the back of the diary, but I didn't take much notice. I mean, who'd want to poke around in those dungeons when you could play up top in the open air?'

'But the church has been locked up tight, with hoardings round it, for ages and ages.'

'I know. Since the end of the war, until this summer when we got permission to go in. I think that whatever it was, has been hidden there since the end of the war. If I'm right, then it's two things, they're very heavy, and they'll fetch a fortune in scrap metal. I think that Mike has discovered where someone hid the bells from the church.'

'What? You mean Mike would go to all this trouble for two silly old bells? You must be off your rocker!'

'I told you, they're worth a lot of money. Enough money to give him and his pals a really good holiday abroad. And we know that he's after something that will do just that, don't we?'

'Yes . . . but . . . bells! I mean . . . boring!'

'They're still buried treasure. They've been buried down under our feet somewhere in the crypt, for all these years. When I went down there with Fats just now, I could hear a sound like "chink, chink". I think it was Mike and Lewis, working with hammer and chisel to uncover the hiding place of the bells.'

'But how would he know where to look?'

'Well, Mr and Mrs Gaunt practically told us that, right at the beginning. We call Skinny "Old", don't we? How's Old Skinny, we say. His father was called Old Skinny, too. Mr Gaunt said that he thought Old Skinny had stolen the bells and hidden them somewhere after the church was bombed, and before it could be made safe against thieves. I think he was referring to our Skinny's grandfather, who was found dead of a heart attack behind the wheel of a stolen lorry, according to Mrs Gaunt. I think Skinny's grandfather, helped by his fifteen year old son, got the bells down from the tower, and until they could borrow or steal a lorry, they hid them in the crypt. Perhaps they put them in a cupboard and screwed up the door, or put them in a recess, and built up a wall of brick or rubble in front of them. Skinny's grandfather died before he could get them out – perhaps he was on his way to get them when he died.

'Now his son, our Skinny's father, went missing for some years, and came back with his brains scrambled. He couldn't remember which way up he was, but he must have remembered enough about hiding the bells to give Mike the idea of looking for them when the site was opened up this summer. I think Mike's got the Warden's old war diary, and with the aid of the plan, he's been searching for the bells. That's why he moved into the Wasteland and set up a lookout post in the shack. That's why he warned us off, and invented the ghost.'

'If that's true,' said Fats, 'then what about poor old Skinny? Our Skinny, I mean. He's down there, and at Mike's mercy!'

'I'm worried about him, too,' admitted Toby, 'but I'm not sure that . . .'

'What are we waiting for?' demanded Nikki. 'How dare Mike frighten us like that! Come on, kids! Let's go down there and give him such a fright that . . .'

'Hold on,' said Toby. 'How do you propose to get through the grille? I can't see any way of . . .'

'Easy,' said Fats. 'My guess is that the only member of the gang who's up top has got the key. What price a raid on Ricky in the shack?'

'We couldn't!' gasped Red.

'Oh yes, we could!' said Nikki. 'He's not looking for any aggro from us. He thinks we're well and truly squashed, and so we were! We've been around all morning, helping your father, Red, and he's taken no notice of us at all. So if Jan and Clare and I go rushing across after a ball, or something like that, he won't think anything of it till he's rolling in the dirt, and then we'll be ever so apologetic, and pick him up and dust him down . . .'

'. . . and I'll pick his pockets for him and get the key!' said Jan. She sounded so confident that no-one dared ask if she'd had experience in this field.

'Yes, but . . .' said Toby.

'If he hasn't got the key, then we'll think again!' said Nikki. 'Come on, kids!'

The three girls rushed off, followed more slowly by Red.

'You don't look all that happy,' observed Fats.

'N-no. Not sure why, but . . . I must admit I can't think of any other way to get in. Can you?'

Fats shrugged. They stood where they could see the

girls playing with a stick, throwing it from one to the other. Ricky had actually come out of the shack. He seemed to be pulling it apart. He had started a small fire, and was throwing all the bits of wood and tarpaulin onto the fire. He didn't pay any attention to the girls at all, until suddenly Nikki threw the stick way over his head and she and Jan rushed him.

He went over with a satisfactory thump, and was knocked back down again by Nikki as he struggled to get up. He threw her sideways with one swipe of his big arm, but there were Jan and Clare twittering around him, holding on to him, laughing and saying they were sorry, and hadn't been looking where they were going. The two girls danced round and round him, and Jan even whipped off his jacket to give it a dust down, clever girl that she was!

Nikki looked a bit shaken, and after a minute or two she walked quietly back to join her brother and Fats. She had a bumpy place coming on her cheek. Fats and Toby eyed her respectfully, but knew better than to say they were sorry.

Jan, Clare and Red came running up a minute later, and dragging the other two into the tower, they displayed their find: a large iron key, about the length of Jan's hand.

' 'Seasy!' boasted Nikki.

'Jan, you're just brill!' said Clare.

Toby had an uneasy feeling that events were moving out of control. Nikki sprang down the steps to the crypt. He wanted to warn her to move quietly, to take Mike by surprise, but Jan and Clare and Red were following on her heels, all chattering away. Fats shrugged and went after them. Toby looked up at the sky, and said to Jesus, 'Sorry about this! Keep an eye on us, will you?'

By the time he got to the bottom of the steps, Nikki was pulling the grille open. Jan and Clare slipped through, closely followed by Red. Everything was pitch black within.

Now was the time to be as quiet as mice.

Nikki fell over something, and screeched her head off.

'Oh, no!' thought Toby, feeling his way along the grille and into the darkness beyond.

'Hush!' said one of the other girls, loudly.

Toby froze. Everything was quiet.

Too quiet.

When he'd been down here with Fats earlier, there had been all sorts of tiny noises. Chink, chink was only one of them. There'd been a soft purry noise, which he'd thought might be some sort of paraffin lamp. Then there'd been the very faint scratchy sound of music, playing in the distance. And street noises in the distance above, of course.

He could still hear the street noises, but the rest had gone missing. It was too quiet.

A listening, breathing sort of quiet.

One of the girls giggled, close by. Toby could hear them scuffling along the passage. He couldn't think why they weren't frightened. He was. Very frightened. He could feel his heart go bang, bang, and he had to work to keep his breathing regular.

'Here's that stupid old curtain!' whispered one of the girls, and then . . . and then a hard, cruel light sliced across the passage.

Clare had lifted the curtain to reveal what lay beyond.

A pickaxe, and some big hammers and chisels lay close by on the floor. There were two sleeping bags there, already rolled up, and a big cardboard box full of cooking equipment. A camper's paraffin stove had been kicked over, and left on its side. Beer cans, Coke cans and fish and chip papers lay around, together with a litter of comics, newspapers, cigarette packets and butts. On the rickety chair nearby a radio stood, but it wasn't playing at the moment.

The light came from a large lamp which was directed full into the eyes of Hawkeye and Co.

'You were right, Toby,' whispered Fats.

'Yes,' groaned Toby. 'I wish I wasn't, don't you?'

Behind them came the clang of the grille shutting fast, and a key turned in the lock. Nikki had overlooked something important, and left the key behind.

'Well, well,' said Mike, who'd been lurking in the darkness beside the grille for them all to walk into his trap. 'A herd of elephants couldn't make more noise than you lot. Well, you can't say you weren't warned, can you? And now you're here, you can save me getting my hands dirty. You're just in time to clear the rubble and get the bells out for us!'

11

Mike pushed them forward into the lighted area, and pulled the curtain down behind him. It was a heavy curtain, made of what looked like two large blankets. It had been tacked to battens on the ceiling and down the right hand wall. It closely swept the other wall and trailed along the floor.

'Scream all you like now,' said Mike, with an evil grin. 'Nobody won't hear you through the curtain. We know. Skinny's tried it.'

He stopped grinning, and thrust them forward again. He was a big lad, was Mike. Nobody would ever nickname him 'Skinny'.

'What are you doing down here?' said Toby, trying to straighten his knees, which wanted to give way and drop him on the floor.

'Looking for buried treasure, a course! Din't you lot work it out, then? Our dad was always telling us of the clever things he did when he were a nipper, along o' *his* dad and uncle in the war. Got away with loadsa stuff from houses that had been bombed. Easy pickings. They got the lead off the roof of this church, the night after it was bombed, and took it away in a lorry they'd borrowed for the purpose.

'They come back the next night for the bells. Uncle was in the building business, and knew where he could sell them. They worked all night. They couldn't just drop the bells down through the trapdoors in the tower, in case they broke. That's what they'd have done, if they were selling for scrap, and it would have been quicker and easier. But no, they had to do it proper, if they was going to sell them.

'So they took the clappers off the bells and lowered them with their tackle, onto a piano remover's trolley. They got as far as the door with the bells, only then the all clear went, so they had to hide the stuff in a hurry. Our dad always said they'd hidden them in the crypt, but that didn't make no sense to me. How could they get those heavy bells, what took two or three men to lift, down the stairs into the crypt? When I usedta ask him that, he'd say he din't know, 'cos he was acting lookout at the time, but that was what Grandad had told him. Our dad said as they'd planned to go back the next night and fetch the bells out but his dad had to take the borrowed lorry back to where he'd found it . . . and he never come back.'

'He had a heart attack, Mrs Gaunt said.'

'Ah, we reckoned he'd strained hisself, lifting all that lead, and the bells being heavy, too. That was the first bit of bad luck, and then the Draft Board caught up with uncle, and he went off to the Army and never come back. Our dad come back to look for the bells soon as he could, but the place had been fenced off with barbed wire, and that Warden was prowling around, so he had to leave it. Then the police come round asking questions about the lead, and he decided to make hisself scarce for a bit . . . and one thing led to another and he din't come back for a long time . . .'

'In prison, was he?'

'Maybe,' frowned Mike. 'That's none of your bizzy. He had a bad time, and it din't do his head no good. Sometimes he couldn't even remember which side of the street he'd lived on as a kid. He'd talk about his "buried treasure" now and then, but it was all mixed up with what he'd do when he won the pools and that. I din't take much notice till little brother here found the diary and I got to thinking there might be something in it, arter all.'

'Skinny found my diary?'

' 'Snot your diary. Finders keepers. Skinny tole me

he'd read it, up in the tower in the summer, and he said there was a plan of the crypt, showing a chute, where they used to tip a load of coke from the path round the church right down into the crypt to feed the boiler.

'So then I thought, Maybe that's how Grandad got rid of the bells – down the chute. But the chute was covered over long ago, when they bulldozed the site to bring down the bits of walls that were still standing. We knew roughly where the chute had been, but we couldn't dig it out with you lot milling around this summer, playing you was a lot of yuppies. Enough to make you sick. What we needed was a set of keys, so we could get in and have a look round inside when it was quiet, like. We followed that old fool Gaunt in here early this week, to see if we could jam a lock open or someping, but he caught me and shouted he was going for the police. So I chased him and the stupid old goat slipped and fell on the stairs . . . and dropped the keys at my feet.'

'So you copied the keys and . . .'

'Nar. You can't copy those old keys. We put a new padlock and chain on the side door and took the key for the grille off the key-ring and made Skinny drop the rest of the bunch into the surgery. We din't think anyone would notice, and they din't, did they?'

'Only you had to make sure we didn't interfere, so you invented the ghost . . .'

'You like it?' A tall dark figure of a man wavered into the light, legs and arms dangling.

Nikki and the other girls screamed, and even Toby and Fats took a step back.

Mike fell about laughing. Lewis, Mike's big black friend, stepped into the light, grinning, and they saw he was holding a dummy mounted on a broom-handle. The 'ghost' had stiff wires through its arms and legs which would keep it steady in any position.

'That's very clever,' said Toby, short of breath. 'Only now we know all about it, you'll have to give up and leave.'

'Not on yours,' said Mike, still grinning. 'We're almost finished. Once we knew where to look, we found the bells quick enough, under the coke pile in the boiler room. The doors of the chute musta blown open when the bomb struck, 'cos the fixings were broke and shored up with timber. We dug the bells out and got them crated up. There's only two struts holding up the chute doors now, and when we pull them away . . . Bingo! The bells go out the way they come in.'

'If there's so much earth and rubble covering the chute, then it'll make a lot of noise when it falls in,' said Toby, taking heart. 'Someone will hear it, or see what's happening, and tell.'

'Not with the hoardings all mended,' said Mike, gloating. 'Not with everyone knowing we're on the site with our telly and radio and that, larking around. Tonight when Mr Red's finished, we take down one section of the hoarding, drive our lorry onto the site, and lift the bells out with a proper building tackle. We've got it all planned. It's taken longer than we'd thought cos one of us had to stay on guard up above all the time, to make believe we was just squatting in the shack. But little brother here helped, din't he? He fooled you nicely, eh? He's been in on this from the beginning, ain't yer, Skinny, me lad?'

At Lewis's side was a woebegone and battered figure. Skinny had lost weight that week. One of his eyes was almost shut, and there were scratches and puffy marks on his face. He had no shoes on.

'Skinny fooled you into thinking hhhe was hiding out from me, and that our mum was bringing him food. All that time he was keeping lookout for us! He scared you good and proper with our ghost, too. Din't you, Skinny?'

Skinny didn't answer, so Mike, still grinning, reached out and twisted Skinny's ear. Skinny squeaked, and said, very fast, 'Yes, Mike! I did what you said!'

'Right!' said Mike, his mock-jovial smile vanishing.

'Let's get to work. There's going to be a lot of rubble to be cleared away from under the chute once we pull the doors open, and since you've chosen to join us, you might as well lend a hand . . .'

Suddenly there was a muffled clanging at the grille. Everyone turned into statues. Three short clangs were followed by three long ones.

'Ricky's signal,' said Mike to Lewis, counting. 'Keep the kids here while I find out what he wants.'

He pulled back the curtain, and disappeared. The murmur of voices came back from the grille round the corner.

'He'll be telling Mike how we got the key off him,' said Fats quietly to Toby. 'Shall we rush him, all of us together?'

'No use,' said Skinny, in a tired voice. 'That's why he never unlocks the grille. You can't get out. I've tried.'

Mike came back, grinning. 'Good news. That was Ricky, wanting to know if he'd left the key in the lock, which he had, the stupid fool.'

Toby didn't dare look at the girls, but sent up a prayer of thanks that at least the theft of the key had not been discovered. He didn't like to think of Mike giving the girls the same treatment he'd given Skinny.

Mike spoke above their heads to Lewis. 'Ricky says Old Man Red's nearly finished. He asked Ricky where the kids had gone. Ricky did the right thing for once. He said the kids had got tired of helping, and went off down the river to play. Old Man Red thinks you and I've gone already, and that Ricky's only staying till a friend brings his lorry to collect our bits and pieces. Mr Red's so pleased we're going of our own accord that he's offered to leave a section of hoarding open for us to get our lorry in and out. He says he'll come back later and close it up. He's gone off now, so we can bring the lorry onto the site as soon as we like. We'll be out of here by supper.'

'What about us?' said Nikki, in a small voice.

'Why, you'll have to stay down here till we're well away,' said Mike, grinning in his evil way. 'No-one won't hear you, no matter how much you scream. But if you're very good and helpful, maybe we'll send a postcard to your mum telling her where to look. They tell me you don't die of starvation under a week.'

Nikki gasped, and Clare moaned. Fats opened his mouth to protest and Mike hit him, spinning him right round so that he fell to the ground. 'To work!' said Mike. 'And fast! We haven't any more time to waste.'

He pushed them through the main room where they'd stored all the play equipment that summer, and into one of the smaller siderooms, empty except for a lot of dark shadows. The ceiling here was held up by massive brick piers, arched in long, low sweeps that seemed to press down on their heads.

The children stumbled along, awkward in the gloom. Red grazed his leg, and moaned, standing on one foot till Lewis growled at him and shoved him headlong through a long, low doorway and down a passage.

Lewis brought up the rear, carrying the large, portable light with him. He held it high, sending their shadows chasing down the passage before them. Red began to sob with pain.

An arched glow showed where the passage came out into another room, which already had a light in it. They tumbled out into what had once been a boiler room, long abandoned to spiders and rats. It stank of dead things.

At the far end was a slide of dull, spider-webbed coke, fused together with age. Pickaxes lay about, showing where Mike and Co. had attacked the pile of coke to extract the bells. There they stood, wrapped in the mouldering remains of sacks, and then cased in new timber frames, all roped up and waiting to be lifted out from the darkness in which they had lain for so long. They were bigger than Toby had expected, one being nearly a metre high and the other only a little smaller. Mr Gaunt had said the bells were called Peter and Paul:

Toby wondered which was which.

They edged into the room round the piles of rubble which had been blown down into the boiler room when the bomb struck, and which Mike and Co. had had to remove from under the shored-up chute doors. Two large joists of timber held the doors closed, but a rope had been attached to them and trailed along the floor, ready for the one last strong pull which would clear the way to the open air and freedom.

Toby tried to think where they were in relation to the world above. He thought they might be almost under his bedroom window . . . and in that case, the chute must be under the floor of the shack. No wonder Mike had left someone on guard all the time!

Lewis propped the portable light on a high ledge above a strongly built but now rusty iron boiler.

Mike said, 'Now to work, kids. Take a hold of that rope and when I give the word, you pull those props away and . . .'

'No,' said Toby. 'I won't help you rob the church, no matter what you do to me.' He said it mildly, but firmly. He was amazed at how little fear he felt.

'What!' Mike raised his arm to hit Toby, and Fats stepped between.

'Don't hit him!' said Fats. 'You don't know him. He gets asthma, any slightest thing. You can't hit him. He might just drop down dead, or something. I'll do his share for him. You just watch me. You don't need him.'

Toby felt a lovely warmth close around him. Fats maybe didn't look as beautiful as Jesus, but he sure had the same ideas about giving his life for his friends.

'Look!' said Fats, picking up the rope. 'I'm twice as strong as him. Out of the way, Toby. Get back down the passage. There's no room for you in here.' He winked at Toby, who obediently backed out into the passage. Toby realised that Fats was giving him a chance to escape, but how could he, with the grille locked?

'Everyone out into the passage, taking the rope with you,' ordered Mike. 'Or we won't have enough room to pull the props away.'

He took the end of the rope, and gestured to the others to follow suit. Now Toby was backed further from the light, with Mike treading on his heels, followed by the others. Lewis was at the doorway when Mike called out to stop.

'Now when I yell, we all take the strain, right? One, two, three . . . heave! One, two, three, heave!'

There was a grinding, screeching sound from the timbers holding up the roof, and Mike shouted out, 'That's it, keep at it! One, two, three, heave! We're nearly there! One, two, three . . .'

There was another ear-battering screech, and they all fell back down the passage as the timbers came loose. Before they could pick themselves up, there was a horrid grinding sound, as the doors gave way. Stones and earth together began to tumble down into the cellar with a terrifying roar.

Toby was thrown back against the wall and even Mike blenched. Screams blended with clouds of dust and the light dimmed. Toby found he couldn't breathe properly. He opened and shut his eyes and mouth, but his chest wouldn't take in any air.

Nikki! He thought. Fats . . . Red . . . He tried to call out, but his voice wouldn't come. He could hear his own breathing, in and out, harrr . . . harr!

Someone was swearing. Someone else was crying. At least two people were coughing. The lights hadn't both gone out. The clouds of dust began to settle.

Mike was doing a lot of the swearing, pulling Nikki out of the passage, and thrusting her back into Toby's arms. Nikki was sobbing. She held onto Toby, and he held on to her.

Toby could see Mike sort of wading through the bodies in front of him, to get to the boiler-room. Fats surfaced, gritting his teeth at the pain in a grazed shoulder. Red, holding his head. The two girls Jan and Clare, whimpering and filthy, but otherwise unharmed.

Lewis was half sitting, half leaning against the door, looking sick. Something had struck his shoulder and he was holding it.

Now Toby could see that the boiler-room door had been pushed almost shut by the piles of rubble that had fallen into the boiler-room.

Mike was trying to push the door open, but it wouldn't shift. He couldn't get through it, either. He pulled Skinny up, and tried to get him through it, but not even Skinny could inch through that tiny space.

Someone was calling down to Mike. It must be Ricky, up above. Probably Ricky had been as shocked as they all were, when the earth opened up at his feet.

Mike shouted up that they couldn't get out that way, and were the bells all right.

Ricky shouted down that he could see the bells, and they looked all right, wrapped up and surrounded by a timber framework as they were. The lorry had just come, and they could easily get the bells out now. Mike and Lewis would have to go back through the grille, though, if they couldn't get back into the boiler-room from below.

'We'll do that, then,' said Mike. He pulled Lewis to his feet, and shook him. Lewis looked as if he didn't know which day of the week it was.

'Useless!' said Mike. 'OK, Fats! You'll have to help us. We need someone to climb down from above, to attach the lifting gear to the bells. The rest of you stay here. I'm not taking any chances. And Fats . . . just you behave or your friends get it, see?'

Mike and Lewis trampled through them, taking Fats. They blundered back down the passage in the dark, cursing. Their only remaining light was stuck on the other side of the door, in the boiler-room. Toby, Nikki and the others followed as quietly as they could, feeling their way along. They moved more slowly than Mike, and by the time they got to the main room, they could hear the grille being locked against them.

12

Toby said, 'Nikki, have you still got your torch?' His breathing was still bad, and the words came out in gasps. Nikki switched on her torch, and they felt better at once. They didn't look better. They looked like nothing on earth, but they were all in one piece.

Toby said, 'Where's Skinny?'

He wasn't with them. Red said, 'Good riddance.'

Toby shook his head. 'Listen, if you had a brother like Mike . . .'

'I'm here,' said Skinny, from the shadows. He dragged himself forward, looking even more bedraggled than before. He said, 'I know you won't hardly believe me, but I'm sorry about this. I never meant it to happen. I never meant none of it to happen.'

'OK, Skinny. I know.'

'No, listen! I got to tell you how it was. I bunked off school, see. I knowed I oughtn't, but I did. I'd seen Mike and his lot come down here, following old Gaunt, and I thought they was going to mug him. I followed them, not daring to let them see me or anything . . .

Skinny drew in a big breath, and shuddered. 'It's so cold down here. I'm never going to feel warm again.' Toby put his arm around Skinny and tried to warm him with his own body.

'. . . but they didn't mug him. It would've been better if they had, wouldn' it?'

'Did you see the accident?'

'No. I heard them talking and saw old Gaunt lying on the floor. He looked dead. It gave me a fright. They heard me and dragged me out. I said I'd come looking for things you'd left here, the binoculars and the diary.

I couldn't say I'd followed them. They'd have done me over. Mike knew about the diary, 'cos I'd told him way back in the summer, how we'd found it and about the plan of the crypt. I didn't mean no harm. Only he'd been interested, and asked me questions, and I was so glad he weren't going to hit me or anything . . . so I told him everything I knew. You would have, too, if you'd been in my place.'

Toby nodded. He probably would.

'So I showed him the diary, and I thought then maybe he'd let me go, but he said I might grass on him, that he couldn't risk it. So he made me stay and help him, instead. And I didn't want to, Toby, honest!'

'I believe you, Skinny.'

'He sent me to the surgery with the keys and a message about Mr Gaunt having had an accident, but Lewis was right behind me, and I knew I'd catch it if I didn't do it exactly as they said. Then they said they were moving in, and I could stop down here till they'd got the bells out. They made me keep watch for them, and they rigged up the curtain and the lights and I had to help search and cook for them and everything.'

'The grille wasn't locked all the time, though. You came up to the church for the doc's talk.'

'They sent me up to see what was going on. Only they took me shoes so's I couldn't get far. And they said I was to go straight back down. I did what they said because I wanted to warn you to keep away in case you got trapped like me. But you didn't listen, and now look what's happened!'

'OK. It's nice to know how it happened. No-one's blaming you. So how do we get out of here?'

'We can't,' said Skinny, in a tired little voice. 'I've tried. The grille's too strong. There's nothing we can do.'

Toby thought that there was. He began to pray. At first his breathing was irregular, and the words came into his head in snatches. Lord Jesus, help . . . and help the others . . . comfort Skinny . . . poor Old Skinny, what it must be to live in fear . . . and his mum, too, I expect. Don't let them take the bells away. The bells should be the voice of the church. How dare they!

Nikki had dropped into a corner, holding Jan in her arms. Clare was sitting with Red, both looking as if they were going to collapse and die. All of them were filthy.

'Isn't there anything we can do, Toby?' said Nikki, trying to wipe her face clean with her handkerchief, and only making matters worse.

'Yes, there is,' said Toby. 'We can pray.' He could feel the others all looking at him, and thinking he was daft. He didn't care. Praying was the only thing to do.

It wasn't going to take long for Mike to get the two bells out, especially if they had proper lifting tackle, and Fats to help them. That patch of ground wasn't overlooked by anybody but Toby when he was up in his bedroom. There wouldn't be anyone in his bedroom now. None of the other windows in the street overlooked that part of the Wasteland. Not even his mum's.

He wondered what his mum would be cooking for their supper. He wondered if the doc would think of searching the Wasteland, when he learned they were missing.

Yes, but the bells would be long gone by then.

He went back to praying. Suddenly he felt different. Someone else was praying, too. That was it. The place was filling up with prayer. Fats was probably praying, up top. Yes, of course. But maybe more than Fats. Maybe even Red, and possibly Skinny. Toby looked around, and saw them all sitting with closed eyes.

Toby wasn't frightened any more. He didn't think the others were, either. That was where they'd gone wrong, right from the beginning. They'd just gone in and done what seemed right to them, but they hadn't asked for help . . . until it was almost too late.

They heard a faint clang from the direction of the grille.

'Sh . . . he's coming back. Maybe he'll let us out if . . .'

'Hush!' Toby switched off the torch, and they waited in the darkness until they heard the grille clang again. Someone came shuffling along the passage and felt his way through the muffling blankets. Toby switched on the torch. It was Fats. He was limping, and there was a trail of blood down his face. He held up his hands, helplessly.

Fats said, 'Ricky was up top, with a big lorry with proper lifting gear on it. They made me climb down into the hole and fix a big hook on the end of a steel hawser to the frames round the bells. There was a lot of rubble and stuff, but the lifting gear took the bells out as clean as a whistle. It didn't hardly take any time at all. I thought they was going to leave me there, down in the hole but they got me up. I suppose they thought I might attract the attention of a passer-by, shouting, or something.'

'They didn't leave the key in the lock, did they?' said Nikki.

'No, I checked.'

'Did you get the licence number of the lorry?'

'Sure. The first three letters are NWR. It's one of McGregor's old lorries. You know, the builders. One of their men bought it when they got a new lorry, and though he's painted over the sign on the side, you can still see the words, faintly. He's that big, fat, hairy chap, the one that got the sack for stealing. He reminded Mike it was Saturday, and they could stop off overnight at the yard, and transfer to another vehicle tomorrow.'

'At least we know where they're going to be tonight.'

'A lot of good that is,' said Jan, sniffling.

'We can tell the police, when we get out.'

'We're never going to get out!' wailed Clare. 'He's left us here to die!'

'Hush, now,' said Nikki. 'But Toby, how can we get out?'

'We will,' said Toby, who did indeed feel confident that they would. 'So, Skinny . . . where's the diary, eh? The Warden would have turned in his grave, if he'd known his diary had helped Mike steal the bells. Let's see if he's got any words of wisdom for us.'

Skinny scrabbled the diary out of the cooking utensil box, and handed it to Toby. The others crowded round, and Toby began to read aloud.

Time flickered on. Occasionally Fats turned his wrist to look at the illuminated dial of his watch. Jan moaned now and then, and Nikki went round, trying to scrub everyone's faces clean with her handkerchief.

Toby turned another page. It was boring stuff, this. All about the Warden's allotment, and his new rose bushes, and how many hours he'd put in fire-fighting, and training . . . and how Old Gaunt – would that have been their Mr Gaunt's father? – had given him a telling-off for borrowing the church keys overnight . . .

'Dead boring!' said Nikki. 'And I'm hungry!'

They all were. And tired. And thirsty. And getting cold.

Toby read on, quietly, but the rest of them started talking, thinking up schemes to get out. Nikki took the other girls through the curtain and started yelling for help. You could hardly hear them, through the curtain. You couldn't hear any noise of traffic.

Toby turned another page. Was the torch getting dim? He hunched nearer.

The Warden said there'd been a bit of bother with a stray dog. Mr Gaunt wouldn't let the keys out of his keeping any more, and they couldn't be duplicated because they were such old, heavy keys. This stray dog had belonged to a household that had got bombed out and the dog had been left behind somehow when the family had moved away. The Warden had found a family to adopt it, but the dog insisted on following him around.

Every time someone went into the crypt, the dog would contrive to get in, too, and hide till dusk, when he'd set up such a barking and whining that you'd think he was being tortured to death. The Warden couldn't bear to leave him barking, but couldn't always get hold of Mr Gaunt to let him out. What a joke on old Gaunt, wrote the Warden, to think how easy it was . . . Toby couldn't read the next few words. Damp and the passing years had caused the page to disintegrate.

Toby thought, Well, Mike couldn't read the words, either. If he'd been able to decipher the words, he wouldn't have left the book for Toby to read. If only he could work it out!

Some words came into Toby's head, but he couldn't be sure who had put them there. Perhaps the Warden had. Perhaps he'd dreamed them.

It couldn't be true, could it? Could it really be as simple as that?

13

The torch was definitely fading. If he wanted to make sure, he'd have to move fast.

'Fats, Red, Skinny. Bring all the cooking things, anything metal you can find, and all the greasy chip papers . . . to the grille, quick!'

They scattered to collect the things and followed him through the curtain to where the girls were crowding about the grille. The girls were hoarse from shouting and ready to cry from frustration.

Toby held the torch up to the grille, but not to the end which was locked. He held the torch to the hinges, to those ancient thick pins of iron on which the gate was hung. Years ago a smith had wrought those heavy gates. They didn't use modern hinges for such gates. They welded large iron rings to the first upright of the grille, and dropped them over pins as thick as a man's thumb which protruded from the wall.

The Warden had written how easy it was *to lift the grille from its hinges!*

Was it really possible! Could the gate really be lifted off its pins, without their having to touch the lock?

The gate was so heavy and large that it looked impossible, but if the Warden had done it unaided, then it could be done.

'We've got to lift the gate off its hinges at this end,' said Toby.

'What?'

'He's off his rocker!'

'No, it's quite possible. Fist we tap the rust off the gate and off the pins. Then we grease them with the chip papers which Mike left behind. Then we use the cooking pan as a lever under this end of the grille, and pack the space with anything that's hard . . . maybe we could break up that old chair and use that. That way we gradually lift this end of the grille up until the rings are clear of the pins that anchor it to the wall. The whole gate should then fall off its hinges. But hurry! The torch is giving out!'

'I see what you mean,' said Fats, examining the pins, 'and I think you're right. It can be done. This frying pan's iron, and might take the weight. Clare, hold up the curtain so's Red and Skinny can search for anything else that's strong enough. Get that chair, will you, Nikki? And let me get at it!'

He tried shifting the grille, but it was fast rusted into place, and even his great strength was not sufficient to move it. Red said he knew what to do, and with Toby holding the torch close, Red tapped away at the rust with an old cooking knife they'd found in the box. They used the greasy chip papers to ease the hinge. Then they all shook the grille hard, to dislodge yet more rust.

Fats tried to lift the gate again, but it had settled firmly into place in the forty-odd years since the Warden had been able to do it single-handed. Then they took Toby's suggestion and began to try leverage. They worked like frenzy, using the frying-pan and the chair legs and seat and back.

The torch faded and went out. Jan stifled a cry, and even Toby felt his courage seep away. They would never get out of there, never!

Toby's eyes adjusted to the light more quickly than the others.

'Look!' he said, pointing up through the grille. A faint grey light came down the winding stair from the church above.

Fats grinned. 'It must still be daylight up there. Funny, I thought my watch had stopped, and we'd been down here all night!'

'We're nearly there,' said Toby. 'You can see, we've

worked the rings almost to the top of the pins. One more go, and we should be out of this . . .'

'Think of supper!' said Nikki, buoyantly.

'Think of a whole bottle of Coke!' said Fats.

Think of the Warden, thought Toby, smiling to himself.

He knew it would work, now. He switched off the now useless torch, but went on praying. 'Help us, Lord . . .'

The gate screeched painfully as it rose that one last centimetre. It teetered on the top of the pins, and fell with a grinding crash on to the stone floor beyond. It was still tethered to the other wall, but at this end it leaned away from the wall at an angle. Even Fats could get through.

As they emerged into the dusk, they heard Mr Red banging the last few nails into the repaired hoarding. They could hear passing traffic. And they could hear Mrs Webb calling for Toby and Nikki.

They looked at one another, and laughed. They were filthy. Some of them had been crying, and that wasn't only the girls.

'I know what my mum's going to say when she sees me,' said Fats. 'She's gonna say, "How many times have I told you not to play with mud!" '

And they all burst out laughing.

So many people wanted to attend the meeting about the future of the church, that in the end they had to hold it in the church itself. Mr Gaunt was back in his old job, looking almost as good as new.

All Toby's gang turned up, and their friends. They sat at the back, and tried not to fidget when the grown-ups pointed them out to one another. Toby and Fats had had their pictures in the local paper only that morning, with a full account of the police action in arresting Mike, Ricky and Lewis before they could dispose of the valuable bells.

The bells themselves had been taken to the police station, and the doc said they'd have to go back to the foundry to be treated before they could be rehung on new rafters in the tower. Toby was looking forward to that.

'Fly away, Peter. Fly away, Paul.
Come back, Peter. Come back, Paul.'

It was only a children's rhyme, but somehow Toby couldn't get it out of his head. He thought the Warden would be happy to have the bells back. Lots of other people would, too.

And talking of lots of other people, he hadn't realised his mum had stirred so many local people up to think about the church and what it could do for the neighbourhood. She was there, of course, with the Beard, and other friends from the Council. The Beard was being very attentive, but Toby was glad to see that she wasn't smiling at him as much as usual.

There were Pakistani families there, and Bangladeshis, and all sorts. Liquorice allsorts, thought Toby in his fanciful way. Liquorice allsorts make a lovely mixture.

Not just one but three men came from Church House to attend the meeting. One was an accountant; you could tell what he was, just by looking at his suit and his briefcase.

Then there was a man pinning up a lot of drawings and photos of churches and buildings. Lastly, there was a nice, smiley man who looked as if he could be pretty tough if he ever stopped smiling, and it turned out he was something high up in the church.

The doc chaired the meeting and introduced the smiley man, who began with a prayer which made some people look a bit embarrassed, but made Toby feel that at least they were starting off on the right foot. Then the man said lots of nice things about the Spirit of the Lord being alive and kicking in their community, and all he had to do was act as midwife.

He said that the church people had been wanting to

redevelop the site for years, but there had been very little interest in the scheme on the part of the community. Church House had felt that the existing number of parishioners could easily be accommodated at the church beyond the shopping centre, and that it might be best to pull down the tower and build sheltered housing on the site.

Now, however, there was a feeling that they could serve the community better. Their architect – and here the smiley man bowed at the man with the drawings – had been involed in various similar projects all over the country, and had brought along photos and drawings to show them what had been done elsewhere.

What they proposed was to retain, restore and extend the tower to serve as a combined community hall and church. Arrangements would be made for someone to come over from the neighbouring parish to take regular services.

'Now we get to the nitty gritty,' said the smiling man. 'I believe the derelict part of the site has attracted the nickname Wasteland. That seems to me very appropriate, because that is actually what it is – wasted land.

'We have been looking at proposals to develop this site for housing purposes, perhaps retaining the crypt for community use. But the existing crypt simply would not be large enough or suitable in other ways. So we have come up with a better idea. We will develop half the site with a building which will harmonise with the tower and will not be any taller than the original church.

'There will be a new crypt and ground floor complex which will be available for community use, with preference given to Guides, Brownies, Mothers and Toddlers, Playgroups . . . everything which your Youth and Community Worker knows so well how to organise . . .' and here he bowed and smiled directly at Kate.

Toby thought, He's done his homework, hasn't he?

'There will be flats above, intended for sheltered housing. One of the flats will be allocated to a live-in caretaker for the complex . . .'

There was a lot about how this would be financed and run, but Toby had got the fidgets, and at last the smiling man turned to him and asked if he had a question.

'Yes,' said Toby, breathlessly. 'The rest of the site . . . can't it be a garden, the Warden's Garden, for everyone?'

'Waste of space,' muttered Jeff, with a dark look.

'Lovely idea,' said all the older people around. 'Just what we need!'

'Yes,' said the smiling man. 'That's rather what we had in mind. Keeping the balance, green spaces, and so on. In fact, your good friend the doctor here put that proposal up to us some time ago, and we agreed in principle . . .'

Toby thought, Marvellous! He slid down in his seat, and didn't take much notice of the rest of the proceedings.

Roses, he thought. Maybe they could grow some of those the Warden had liked so much. And there'd be a grassy bit for the old people to sit on, and maybe a small playground and bushes and bulbs and weeds. There'd always be weeds. You couldn't get round that. But they'd keep watch and pull out the weeds as they came up.

When the meeting was over, his mum went over to talk to the doc. Jeff tried to grab her, but she didn't seem to see him. She looked at the doc as if she wasn't sure he would want to talk to her, but of course the doc did. Soon they had their heads together, and Toby heard her say Jeff didn't understand how highly strung and delicate Nikki was . . .

That gave Toby the giggles. He went outside into the cool darkness of the night. Fats lifted a hand and went off with his family. Red and Skinny were walking Clare home, and Jan got in a huddle with Nikki, planning some outing or other.

Toby went through a newly-created gap in the hoarding, into the Wasteland. It was odd about that. The people hereabouts seemed to think they owned the Wasteland, and had a right to go into it whenever they wanted. The newly-repaired hoarding had had a gap torn in it within a couple of days of Mr Red leaving the site.

From where he stood, Toby could see the lighted church, with people still hanging around the door. Lights and bells, he thought. It had taken a long time to get the church operating again, but they were gradually getting there.

The local lads had found the fake 'ghost' figure and had set it up nearby for target practice. The helmet had fallen under a bush. Toby rescued it, and turned it round and round in his hands, wondering how Mike had come by it, and what adventures it had been through in its time.

Mr Gaunt hailed him from the pavement. 'Why, Toby! You gave me quite a turn. I thought it was the Warden, back again. Many's the time I seen him standing there, turning his old helmet round and round, talking about getting the church rebuilt, or about his roses.'

'Now come along, you,' said Mrs Gaunt. 'It's getting late, and you only just out of your bed. . .'

She took him off, and Toby stood there, looking down at the helmet. Did Mr Gaunt really think that he, Toby Webb, was carrying on where the old Warden had left off?

His mum stopped at the entrance long enough to yell at him to come home. The doc was with her. Toby dropped the helmet where he'd found it. Then he changed his mind, picked it up, and carried it off with him. It would remind him to ask for help from the right quarter when things went wrong.